D0282552

Dancing Leaf

CHARLOTTE JANE ELLINGTON

The Overmountain Press
JOHNSON CITY, TENNESSEE

ISBN 13: 978-1-57072-311-7
ISBN 10: 1-57072-311-7
Copyright © 2007 by Charlotte Jane Ellington
Printed in the United States of America
All Rights Reserved

1 2 3 4 5 6 7 8 9 0

To my mother, Marion Blattner
And to the memory of my father, Paul Blattner

NOTES AND ACKNOWLEDGEMENTS

Dancing Leaf is a work of historical fiction. Various characters in the novel, however, are authentic personages from the Cherokee world of the 1820s—Nancy Ward, Long Fellow, Five Killer, the Ridge family, Father and Mother Gambold, and Sequoyah.

Nancy Ward's home on the Ocoee River, the Ridges' plantation, the Cherokee council grounds, and the mission school at Spring Place are all noted locales of the time period.

The myths that precede each chapter of the novel are genuine Cherokee myths passed down in oral tradition by storytellers. My own telling of the stories was adapted from various sources. I have listed below the myths by chapter and title as they appear in *Dancing Leaf,* followed by the credited source from which they were derived.

Chapter 1 "Sun and Moon" and Chapter 11 "Why Turtle's Shell Is Scarred" are found in *Walking on the Wind: Cherokee Teachings for Harmony and Balance* by Michael Garrett, Bear & Company, a division of Inner Traditions International, Rochester, Vermont, 1998, pages 9-12 and 87-90.

Chapter 2 "Possum's Tail," Chapter 3 "The Uktena," Chapter 4 "The Bear People," Chapter 6 "How the World Was Made," Chapter 7 "The Daughter of the Sun," and Chapter 10 "The Book" are recorded in *Myths of the Cherokee and Sacred Formulas of the Cherokees* by James Mooney from 19th and 7th Annual Reports, Bureau of American Ethnology, reproduced 1982 by Charles and Randy Elder—Booksellers, Publishers, Nashville, Tennessee, pages 269-271, 297-298, 325-326, 239-240, 252-254, and 351.

Chapter 5 "Spider Woman," Chapter 8 "How the Redbird Got His Color," and Chapter 12 "The Legend of the Strawberries" are told in *Medicine of the Cherokee: The Way of Right Relationship* by J. T. Garrett and Michael Garrett, Bear & Company, a division of Inner Traditions International, Rochester, Vermont, 1996, pages 150-153, 79-81, and 157-160.

Chapter 9 "Star Woman" is from *Voices of Our Ancestors: Cherokee*

Teachings from the Wisdom Fire by Dhyani Ywahoo, 1987, pages 29-32, and is printed in adapted form here by arrangement with Shambhala Publications, Inc.

The shamanic prayers in Chapter 5 were adapted from a formula for treating infant diseases found in *Myths of the Cherokee and Sacred Formulas of the Cherokees.*

John Ridge's poem "On the Shortness of Life" in Chapter 8 is archived in the Papers of John Howard Payne, Edward E. Ayer Collection, at the Newberry Library, Chicago.

The letter read by Charles Hicks in Chapter 8 is an adapted form of a letter sent by Samuel Worcester to Charles Hicks, March 4, 1819, recorded by the American Board of Commissioners for Foreign Missions. Its more complete form can be found in *Trail of Tears: The Rise and Fall of the Cherokee Nation* by John Ehle, Doubleday, New York, 1988, page 157.

In Chapter 8 Dancing Leaf's quotes from Beloved Mother's letter to the Cherokee council are from a document found in Jackson Papers Book 29, No. 17, Vol. 14, pages 6452-6453. The entire letter is recorded in *Nancy Ward and Dragging Canoe* by Pat Alderman, The Overmountain Press, Johnson City, Tennessee, 1990, page 80.

The deed to Nancy Ward's property, read by Dancing Leaf in Chapter 11, is an adapted form of the legitimate document of reservation recorded in the United States Archives Record Group number 75. Dancing Leaf, a fictional character, was not the actual heir designated by Nancy Ward; the land was bequeathed to Nancy's granddaughter, Jenny McIntosh. The accurate excerpt of the entry can be found on page 81 in *Nancy Ward and Dragging Canoe.*

The vows exchanged in the Cherokee ceremony of marriage in Chapter 12 are loosely based on sections of a formula for love titled "Concerning Living Humanity (Love)" found on pages 376-377 in *Myths of the Cherokee and Sacred Formulas of the Cherokees.*

A special acknowledgement and note of thanks to my husband, Ed, and to my friends in my writing group—Pat Bates, Linda DeStefano, Donna George, Nancy Hill, Olga Kronn, Janet Minor, and Carol Paquette—who provided valuable advice and encouragement.

CONTENTS

SUN AND MOON

A long time before Elohino, Mother Earth, was as old as she is now, a young man, Iga-e-hinvdo, Sun, lived in the East. Sun was well-loved. He walked the sky every day, brave and true, searching for a magic lake. He knew that when he observed his reflection in the shimmering waters, he would see his true medicine vision. His evenings were spent in the medicine lodge—singing, praying, and listening for the Great One to tell him his purpose.

In the West lived a beautiful young woman, Udosvno-e-hi—Moon—who also was well-loved. She moved calmly and peacefully, always comforting others with her presence, even though she was painfully shy. Moon loved Sun, but Sun was too busy searching for his medicine to take much notice of her.

Now, Sun had a lover who came to see him in the dark hours of the evening; she was always gone before morning so that he never saw her face, and she would never reveal her identity. He cherished their time together and yearned for her during the long hours of the day.

One evening, when his lover had dozed off, Sun reached into the fire pit, retrieving ashes. He brushed some of the black ash onto his lover's face, saying, "Your face is so cold."

The next evening, while Sun waited for his lover, he looked up at the night sky, and there he saw Moon's face smudged with ash. Suddenly he knew that Moon was his lover. Moon knew then that she had been found out, and she was deeply embarrassed. From then on, she always tried to stay a long way behind Sun, making herself as thin as a ribbon when he came close.

Still, because of her deep love for Sun, she never washed off the ashy spots. If you look close, you can still see them. Some people say that the stars are glittering tears that trickle from Moon's face when she is thinking of Sun.

And still each day, Sun searches for his vision and for his lover, Moon, who is always on the other side of the horizon.

Chapter 1

I heard the creak of the door as the shaft of light fanned wider. Slowly I turned, and there stood Blue Lake. He did not see me, though, as he stretched his eyes to take in the darkness of the storehouse. He took three steps toward the rows of hanging dried fruits and vegetables. I watched his lips move as he counted them—two rows of cabbage leaves; a row each of dried apples, peaches, and pumpkins; seven bundles of corn.

"We have enough potatoes," I said in a not-too-loud voice. Still, he startled, and when he turned toward me, I bent down and raked again over the pile of potatoes with my stick.

"Dancing Leaf! I didn't know you were in here," he said. "I was just judging how far the supplies will last."

"We have plenty of everything," I said as I stood and flipped my braids behind my back. "If not, we can always buy from others." I separated two potatoes from the rest of the pile. Bending down, I examined them closer. As I had thought, they were completely black and mushy on one side. Without looking at Blue Lake, I gently rolled them out the door with my stick and, with a strong thrust, knocked them into the brush growing beside the path. "Only the polecat smells worse than a rotten potato," I said.

Blue Lake followed me outside. He closed the door and turned the block of wood that held it shut. His rifle was leaning against the wall, and he picked it up and put his arm through the strap. "I'm going to look for the deer, the big one whose hooves I see each morning close to the corn patch. He's waiting for the ears to ripen." He squinted in the sun and looked to the woods across the meadow. "We can dry the meat we don't eat tonight. There should be plenty to last for a few more weeks."

"We have enough now," I said.

But he ignored me and turned to his dog. "Chera, stay. You'll only scare the deer off."

Chera whimpered and looked up at me, as if I might give her permission, but I echoed Blue Lake's command. "No, you have to stay."

We stood and watched as he crossed the field, his back straight and strong, his raven black hair lifting lightly in the summer breeze. With his fringed moccasins, his red sash, and the blue cloth wound round his head, anyone would know that he was a Cherokee brave. But anyone gazing upon his face would quickly see the blue eyes of his father's people. *HB.* Those were the letters behind his name in the black ledger book at the mission school—half-breed. Beside my name were the letters *FB* because I am a full blood.

A rabbit suddenly leapt from a hiding place and darted across the high grass. Chera rose to attention, her ears pitched forward. Blue Lake lifted his rifle and shot, but I saw the zigzag pattern continue across the field and the part of the brush along the edge, and I knew Mr. Rabbit had made a successful escape—or maybe it was Mrs. Rabbit, trying to detract from a nest of young.

Chera whimpered again.

"No," I repeated firmly. "Stay with me." I was glad she was with me, because she, no doubt, would have found the nest. "Come," I said, "you and I will return to the cabin."

Long Fellow was standing on the back porch, smoking his pipe, as Chera and I approached. "How was your nap, Uncle?" I asked.

He lifted his pipe to me and was about to say something when we heard the crack of the rifle. We paused and listened and then heard a war whoop, signaling Blue Lake had accomplished his mission.

"I'll help drag him in," Long Fellow said. He jumped off the porch and hurried in his shuffle run, one knee bending, the other not.

"He should use a walking stick," I complained to Chera, who never argued with me. "He's too stubborn," I added.

The old ones are always stubborn, I reflected as I went in to check the vegetables stewing in the pot. Beloved Mother, my adoptive mother, had been very stubborn the last few years of her life—refusing to lie down for a rest in the afternoon, or insisting she could eat turnips, when every time I would have to rush outside with her in the middle of the night because of the cramping pain. If I tried to persuade her to ride to town in a wagon, she would declare that she must ride on her horse, and the next day would be a day of moaning pain and aching joints.

"I will not be like them when I grow old," I told Chera, although when I said the words, the faces of Catherine and Betsy, Beloved Mother's daughters, appeared in my mind, and I heard their scolding words: *Why are you so stubborn? You should come live with us where you can be with families and other women.*

But I could not leave the home where I had lived with Beloved Mother and her brother, Long Fellow, these past five years. Beloved Mother had died only this past fall. How could I abandon Long Fellow so soon after her death? True, Five Killer, Beloved Mother's son, lived only a stone's throw away, but he had recently brought his new wife to live with him, and Raven was a demanding presence. And yes, Blue Lake, who was like an adopted son to Five Killer, had moved in with Long Fellow and me after Raven's appearance, but Blue Lake was now talking of leaving to be with his natural father. So Long Fellow's care was left to me. Of course, I did not mind caring for Long Fellow; I loved him and wanted to care for him.

I stirred the dried carrots, pumpkin, and apples simmering in the pot and satisfied myself that none were sticking to the bottom. Chera and I were alone in the cabin, and the thought came to me that it would take a good while for Long Fellow and Blue Lake to drag the deer in, and then they would have to hang him and let the blood drain before they cut out the meat for roasting. My eyes searched the room while Chera looked at me, puzzled.

"You, I know, will not tell," I said as I crossed the kitchen. Still, I walked on my toes so there would not be the sound of my foot falling. I pushed aside the curtain in the room where Blue Lake and Long Fellow always slept. Blue Lake's satchel was lying beside the raised bed with his sleeping mat.

I undid the strap, opened the flap, and peered inside. The letter was in there, standing on its side. "I am not a thief or a criminal," I informed Chera, who stared intently at me. "This letter was read to me by Blue Lake himself only three days ago."

Chera lay down, crossing her front paws and resting her head upon them while she continued to stare at me.

"It is just that he read so quickly, and I cannot remember everything the letter said." I thought perhaps I would find more understanding if I reread slowly.

"Dearest William." *William?* I had turned to Blue Lake with startled eyes when he read that.

"It is my Christian name," he had said. "It is the name of my father's father."

"I am not well," he continued reading. "The doctor believes I have a few months yet. I would like to see you before I die. Also there is the matter of my estate. I want you to be a part of it. Please come as soon as possible. I have included a map and directions. Your loving father, Charles."

The *loving father* words had caused the blood to pulse in my head. "A loving father doesn't desert his wife and son," I informed Blue Lake. "What kind of trick could this be? He expects you to travel all the way to Virginia?"

"He wanted me to go with him when he left eight years ago, Dancing Leaf. I was small and wanted to stay with my mother. Besides, it's the Cherokee way—children belong to the family of their mother, not the family of the father."

"Yes, which is why you have stayed with the Cherokee. And when your mother died, why didn't he send for you then?"

"Of course, he didn't know. He started looking for me a year ago. Someone from the old town wrote him and said I was living here with Five Killer in the Amovey district, and that's how I got this letter."

"I see you are happy about this," I said as I stared at the letter he held in his hands. "So, you are going to Virginia?"

"I feel I have to," he answered slowly, refolding the letter. "He is my father. He's dying, he wants to see me, and there's the matter of his estate. If he wants to leave me property, I should be there to claim it."

"Yes, I see, you must go," I said with my mouth, but the words in my head were different: *No, I don't see. To travel to see a man who has cared so little about you is a stupid thing.* "I have to check my fishing basket," I added, abruptly turning from him.

Actually I had not been to the stream to set out my basket trap that day but had gone instead to sit on my favorite rock and listen to the rushing whispers of the water. In the early summer, the water runs clear, and you can see the orange and red of the stones and the stripes and speckles on the backs of the fish that dart about between the growing mosses.

I would have found it easier if Blue Lake had presented the letter with a long face and sorrowing eyes. But no, his eyes danced and a smile flitted lightly across his lips, like a butterfly flutters above a patch of flowers. But as for me, heaviness pressed my heart, as if someone had placed a large stone on it.

And so, in the past three days, since the coming of the letter, Blue Lake had scurried around the farm like a squirrel preparing for winter. He had mended the fences around the vegetable garden and the corn patch. He had carved new bird feeders from the hardened squash rinds of the past fall. He had repaired three boards on the roof of the cabin and made a new stone pathway to the chicken house and the storehouse. He had worked from sunrise to sunset, which left little time for talk between us, and maybe that is why he worked so hard.

Chera barked and ran to the porch. With trembling hands, I returned the letter to the satchel and hurried out. Across the field I saw the two of them—Long Fellow and Blue Lake—dragging a carcass with a dangling head.

When they had it hung from the limb of a tree, Blue Lake cut a piece of meat from the underside and placed it on a spit to roast above the fire. Five Killer came down from his cabin, and the three of them cut long strips and hung them above a smoking fire on the other side of the cabin. The dried meat would serve us for many months. Raven came, too, and together we made cakes of corn bread, which we wrapped in silky corn leaves and placed in the ashes to bake.

When finally we all sat down to eat, Raven talked and talked, describing the hard work of cleaning up the cabin after her long absence. She had only recently returned from Coosa Town, where she had visited with her daughter and her twin grandbabies. I was glad Raven was with us now, because it was Blue Lake's last night with us, and without her, there would have only been the clanking of metal utensils and long sighs and a few utterances from Five Killer or Long Fellow or Blue Lake.

"Are you taking Chera?" Five Killer asked. "It's better to travel with a dog if you have no one else. A dog can be some protection."

"Yes, I will take her," Blue Lake said.

The stone on my heart sank to my stomach. If he took Chera, that meant he had one less reason to return. Besides, I loved Chera. I was the one who had taken care of her when Blue Lake went to the council meeting a year ago.

"Chera will have young before the changing of the moon," Long Fellow said in the same quiet way he would say, "Tomorrow it will rain."

"She will?" Both Blue Lake and I voiced the question at the same time. Blue Lake rose from the table and went over and felt on the underside of her belly.

"Maybe you shouldn't take her then," Five Killer advised. "Who knows what will happen? You can't travel on a horse with a brood of puppies. You can take Blackie," he offered. "He's young and strong."

"No, I couldn't."

Again heaviness pressed my heart, for Blue Lake would surely take Blackie if he planned to come back.

"Go on. Take him," Five Killer insisted. "I'll have one of the new puppies if you don't return."

Ai-yee! I wished he had not said those words aloud.

"Again I must recheck my trap," I said in a rush and hurried out of the room. I ran down to the stream, hoping no one would follow me, yet desperately praying someone would. But I sat alone on my rock and looked back from time to time, to where the three of them stood on the porch, smoking pipes, discussing future days.

It was dark when I returned, and Five Killer and Raven had departed for their own cabin. Long Fellow still stood on the porch, his pipe now cold and resting at his feet.

"Blue Lake has gone to bed," he informed me. "He leaves tomorrow at sunrise."

I nodded and started to go in when Long Fellow called me back. "Dancing Leaf, you should tell him how you feel, what you think about this. Do you want him to go?"

"No matter," I answered. "He's going."

"Well, he may not come back if he thinks there's no reason."

"No matter," I repeated.

"You are a very stubborn child," he persisted.

"I am not a child!" I protested. My voice broke, and tears like the first raindrops of a storm splattered my cheeks. Quickly I went to my room so Long Fellow would not see them streaming down my face.

On my sleeping mat I curled my body tight. Long Fellow's words were piercing darts. If Five Killer had said them, or Betsy or Catherine, it would have been a smaller matter, but Long Fellow uses such few words in a day, and he had never spoken to me before in a scolding manner.

I lay on my mat, making myself as still as could be. I counted my breaths till they became long and even. I listened. I heard nothing from Blue Lake; he always slept quietly. But Long Fellow's breath sounded like the Unaka—the white man—walking on dried leaves. The next day I would make him comfrey tea and insist he drink it before retiring.

Quietly I rose and walked on toes to the big room. Burning embers glowed in the hearth, but no flames remained. I reached for the jar beside the fireplace and took a pinch of tobacco, holding it in my hand as I lifted my mind to the Great One, residing in Galunlati above. What prayer should I offer? I could not say what was in my heart: *O Great One, please make sure that Blue Lake returns to me.* It would not be fair to Blue Lake, who must find his own true path.

I thought about the prayers that Beloved Mother offered, and I remembered that she always began with prayers of thanks, so I gave thanks. Thanks that Five Killer had found me by the running water of the stream many years ago when my village had been destroyed. Thanks that he had brought me to live with Beloved Mother. Thanks that Beloved Mother had chosen me from all of the orphan children and adopted me as her daughter. Thanks for my uncle Long Fellow and my brother Five Killer. And finally I came to Blue Lake. I gave thanks for knowing one so strong and true. And then I asked the Great One to watch over Blue Lake, to guide his steps on the journey, to protect him from bad people. I asked that Blue Lake see his reflection in the magic lake and find his true path in life. And I did not ask for anything more.

I reached in and touched my fingertips on the cooled ashes at the edge of the fire and smudged my cheeks and forehead and nose. Blue Lake and I would be as Sun and Moon in the days that followed. We would be far from each other. Perhaps when he looked at the moon in his nights of travel, he would think of me. I judged that I had done the right thing, these past few days, making myself thin as a ribbon.

I sat and watched until the glow of the embers died. My prayer, I was sure, would be carried by the smoke to the spirit world above. I knew it to be a true and good prayer, for my heart was no longer weighted with stone.

POSSUM'S TAIL

At one time, Possum had a beautiful tail of which he was very proud. He brushed it every night and sang about it every morning. Rabbit, who had no tail at all since Bear pulled it out, was jealous and decided to play a trick on his friend.

When it came time for the great council dance, he said to Possum, "You know your tail will get wet and muddy and be filled with leaves and debris when you cross the river. Let's get Cricket to come over tonight and see what he suggests."

Now, Cricket was the best barber in the kingdom, so Possum was pleased. When Cricket came, Possum stretched out and slept while Cricket brushed his tail and wrapped it tightly with red cloth so it would stay nicely until the dance. But Cricket had been in counsel with Rabbit, and the two had planned some mischief, so all the time Cricket was wrapping, he was also cutting Possum's hair close to the roots. Possum slept peacefully through all of this and awoke the next day, excited to go to the dance.

That evening the animals gathered around the council fire. First the little chipmunks, squirrels, beavers, and other small animals paraded, proudly showing off their tails. Everyone applauded politely. Then it was Possum's turn. The drummers drummed, and Possum unwrapped the cloth as he danced about and sang, "See my beautiful tail! What a fine color! See how it sweeps the ground—such fine fur!"

But the audience did not applaud. Instead, a murmur started and grew louder and louder, and soon Possum realized they were all laughing. When he finally looked down, he saw that his tail was as bare as a lizard's. He fell down with shame and could not say a word or get back up. And even to this day, the possum will roll over and lie still when he is surprised.

Chapter 2

I remained in my bed the next morning until Blue Lake finished feeding his horse in the barn. Only then did I start down the stone path to milk the cow. I searched the sky to judge what kind of day it would be. Red ribbons of clouds wove in and out between the shadows of the hills. In the western sky, a pale ghost moon lingered, and when I returned with a pail of milk, the moon had faded into the mists of morning.

On the path, Blue Lake and I came face-to-face, for he was heading back to the barn, perhaps to retrieve one more thing. I glanced up at him but then turned my eyes back to my moccasined feet, for the stones were slippery with dew. Blue Lake stopped and blocked my path, and when I looked up again, he was staring at me, his eyebrows rising together in the middle of his forehead.

"What's on your face?" he asked as he reached up and brushed my cheek. His hand drew back with smudges of ash.

I quickly reached up; my fingers, too, returned with ash. "It is nothing," I stammered, but my face felt aflame. I wished that the earth would open and swallow me; I would go to live with the Kanatsa people, the Cherokee who fasted and prayed and were taken to live under the river, where they could remain safe from the cruelties of the world. How could I have forgotten to wash the ash from my face? I had washed my hands before milking the cow but had never given thought to my face.

Blue Lake reached for the handle of the pail and said, "Here, I'll take this in while you wash."

But I held on tightly and pulled in my own direction, and some of the milk spilled over the top. "I may not wish to wash my face today," I declared. "And see, you have caused me to spill milk." It was bad enough that Long Fellow and Five Killer treated me like a child at times; I refused to be treated so by Blue Lake. As I made my way up the path, I called back, "Get the wash bucket and rinse the milk off the steps, or they will be sticky."

In the cabin, Long Fellow had already made coffee. I warmed corn cakes and scooped a bowl of berries from the clay pot on the storage shelf. Five Killer came down to eat with us and to say farewell to Blue Lake.

After breakfast, Long Fellow took a map from the deerskin box, and the three of them went out on the porch while I washed the table and put the cooking things in order. When I finished, I took two buckets to the stream to fetch water for the day.

They were still talking when I returned, and they seemed in no hurry, so I retrieved my writing paper, my quill pens, and my gooseberry ink from the deerskin box and sat down to work on my stories. Usually I saved my writing for the afternoon, while Long Fellow napped, but now the three of them were out there, wasting time, none of them working, so I felt no need to occupy myself with chores either. I looked over what I had written before—more than a hundred pages, tied with ribbon.

I had begun my writing when Beloved Mother became weak and sick, and I determined that I should remain with her instead of returning to the mission school. In my heart I knew she would die, and I decided to put the stories of her life on the pages of the talking leaves, which would be something I could keep forever. When I finished, I tied them all up with a white ribbon, for white is the color of peace and happiness. And inside the knot I put a swan feather from Beloved Mother's cape, for her cape of swan wings symbolized her rank of distinction as ghigau, or beloved woman.

For many months after her death, I could not look at the pages, nor could I pick up a pen or a piece of paper. But in the spring, when the earth thawed and the mountain streams were swollen with water, and the summer birds returned and built nests for their young, and the wild roses bloomed along the hillside, then my heart, too, began to thaw, and once again I took up my pen.

Since then I had been writing the stories of our people, the stories told at the council fires and passed on from grandfathers to grandchildren. The stories of how the world was made and how man obtained fire. Of Selu, the first woman, and Kanati, the first Cherokee brave. The stories of the stars and constellations. I wrote about the time the animal kingdom sent diseases to man and the plant kingdom came to our rescue. And I wrote also of the tricks the animals played on each other.

On this day I began to write the story of the possum's tail. I worked quietly as I listened to the voices on the porch. Five Killer unrolled the map and discussed whether to cross the Tennessee River by ferry at John's Landing or whether to travel farther north where the river could be waded if the days remained dry. Long Fellow pointed out the Cherokee towns of Tellico and Coyatee, where friends lived and where Blue Lake could stop for rest and food.

The three of them agreed that Blue Lake should travel the Great War Trace Road to Virginia and then follow the Wilderness Road east. They judged that the entire journey would be a matter of one week if all went well. Finally I heard them rolling up the map, and their feet shifted about on the wooden planks of the porch.

Blue Lake's voice drifted through the window. "Keep her in the cabin until after I've left. Don't let her out. I feel like I'm deserting her. I couldn't bear to see the sadness in her eyes."

At those words, torrents of anger pulsed in my head. I stood up quickly and marched boldly onto the porch, positioning myself in front of Blue Lake. "I will not be kept in the house," I said plainly. "And the expression in my eyes will be one of happiness. I am glad you will be reuniting with your father, Blue Lake."

I crossed my arms in front of my chest and stared at him gravely, but he returned a look of astonishment, and Five Killer burst out laughing. Long Fellow tried not to laugh and, instead, coughed for several minutes while Blue Lake pounded his back.

"He was talking about Chera, not you," Five Killer said when they had quieted.

"Ah," I said, again wishing to fall through a hole in the earth. The sun was not yet at mid-sky, and already twice I had shamed myself. I could think of no words to reclaim my dignity, so I said simply, "I will take Chera in."

They talked in low murmurs for a short while, then Blue Lake's face appeared at the doorway. "I leave now, Dancing Leaf."

Motioning for him to come in, I frowned at the others, hoping they would not follow, but they did. I handed Blue Lake the medicine pouch I had made for him the day before. "This contains snake root for fever and snakebites, milkweed for cuts and scratches, and heartleaf for coughing."

"Thank you, Dancing Leaf," he said, awkwardly holding the pouch in his hand.

I took a step forward and draped it over his head and around his neck. Long Fellow and Five Killer shifted feet and looked down, but neither of them made an excuse to leave. If they were not there, I thought Blue Lake might put his arms around me and pull me close. My heart was beating wildly and I wanted him to, but instead he quickly turned and went out the door and down the steps and mounted his horse.

He held up his hand in farewell, and we watched as his form receded in the distance. He did not go fast because Blackie was trailing behind, a rope attached to his neck. Five Killer was afraid Blackie would object to leaving, but he trotted happily along as if he were off to a great adventure. Chera was the unhappy one; she whimpered from the other side of the door. Her master was leaving without her, but at least she did not see that he had taken someone else with him. When I went in, I comforted her with a strip of deer meat.

I did not feel like other work, so I went back to copying the story of the Possum's tail, one of my favorites. Some of the stories are sad and long, and I do not always understand them. But the animal stories are amusing, and on this day I wished to be amused.

Five Killer went back up the hill to his cabin, and Long Fellow lingered on the porch as was his custom. A short time later, he called to me, "Dancing Leaf, someone is coming—a Unaka. Come see who it is." Long Fellow's eyes were clouded; he could not distinguish forms in the distance.

I stepped out and watched the rider approaching. He was indeed a white man, and there was something familiar about him. When he reached the large pine, which was the length of a ball play field from the cabin, a wave of remembrance swept over me, but still I could not place him.

He lifted his hat and shouted, "Hey, Dancing Leaf. How ya doing there?"

"Jonathan?" I questioned softly, turning to Long Fellow.

Yes, the man was Jonathan Young, but so many things were different. He was at least a foot taller. His hair was long—to his shoulders—and whereas before it was the color of winter grass, it now was the darker tone of bee's honey, and some of it was growing under his nose and on his chin. His voice was round and deep. He wore the clothing of a man—black pants, a white shirt, and a black coat—not the overalls and patched shirt his mother had sewn. The hat he waved was tall and white.

"Well, hey. How are you all?" he greeted as he looped and tied his reins over the post. "I just had to come and talk to you. Ma told me about Gr—" He stopped himself and glanced at me because he had almost said *Granny,* the name he and the other children from the white settlement called Beloved Mother. I had often reproached him for this because "Granny" was not a title of proper respect. "Uh . . . Mrs. Ward," he finished, and I was surprised at his graciousness.

He did not wait for an invitation but quickly mounted the porch, his boots pounding each step. He addressed Long Fellow in a shouting voice that paused after each syllable, "Mr. Long Fellow, I'm sorry to hear about your sister's passing."

Long Fellow did not understand English well, so I translated the words. He nodded to Jonathan and replied in Cherokee, "It is well. Nanyehi has crossed the Milky Way and returned to the lodge of the Creator." This he said not for Jonathan, but for me, because I had grieved for months when Beloved Mother died. He did not want me to grieve any longer.

"He said she lives in heaven now," I informed Jonathan.

Jonathan bowed and said, "I've come to pay my respects. I would like to put flowers on her grave and read a few passages from the Lord's book." He removed a black, bound book from the pocket inside his coat and held it forward for Long Fellow to see.

Again I repeated his words in Cherokee and wondered what Long Fellow would say. He, like other Cherokee men his age, respected the white man's book but did not believe it had a place in Cherokee life. Still, he nodded politely and motioned for Jonathan to sit.

I went inside, scooped water into a cup, and squeezed fresh blackberries. When I returned, Jonathan took the cup and declared, "I don't think little Henry would be with us if it hadn't been for Mrs. Ward."

Beloved Mother had made trips to the home of Jonathan's family for a whole week when Henry was an infant, because he cried with fierce stomach pains, spitting up his mother's milk and producing loose, foul-smelling stools. Beloved Mother had given the baby drops of red juice from the stalk of the skullcap several times a day and milkweed juice at night. On the seventh day Henry had no spitting up and no running stools. The next time we saw him was when Mrs. Young brought Beloved Mother the speckled hens. He was a fat baby then.

"How is Henry?" I asked.

"He's fine. He's walking now, and my sisters have to follow him to keep him out of trouble."

"The grave is a mile from here," I told Jonathan. "Beloved Mother wanted to be buried on a high place where she could see the land below. I will get my horse, and we'll ride."

I went out to the field and whistled so Red Sky would come in. As I fitted the bridle bit in her mouth, my spirit suddenly soared at the thought of visiting Beloved Mother's grave. Nearly a year had passed since her death, and I could now think of her without the pain in my heart. But as I swung my leg over Red Sky's back, small darts of guilt stabbed at me because I couldn't remember the last time I had visited the grave. It must have been in the white man's month of May, when

Blue Lake and I had found the beautiful white rock streaked with orange and gold by the mountain stream. We purified it in the flowing stream and then placed it on top of the other rocks on her grave.

The sun was midway in her daily voyage as Jonathan and I started toward the meadow. The sky was a dome of clear blue with only a few puffs of white clouds. Blue Lake would have a good day for travel, I judged. Jonathan stopped midfield, and I held the reins of his horse while he gathered wildflowers. When he had a large bouquet, he remounted and we rode on.

"I saw Blue Lake as I was riding in," he announced.

"You did?"

"Yes, we stopped and talked for a minute. I told him he'd like Virginia." His eyes looked sideways at me, but I kept mine fixed on the distant hill.

"I asked him if he was planning to come back," he continued, "but he didn't say. What do you think?"

"Only Blue Lake knows his mind."

"Well, how do you feel about it? I bet your family is sorry to see him go. Five Killer especially. Blue Lake and Five Killer have been like father and son."

My body jolted at those words even though Red Sky's step was even. Yes, Blue Lake and Five Killer had lived together for five years as father and son. Perhaps I wasn't the only one grieving his departure.

"Besides," Jonathan added, "I thought maybe you two would get hitched . . . you know, married."

"It is impolite to talk of such things," I retorted quickly, glaring at Jonathan, who kept his own eyes forward now.

I regretted bringing this one to Beloved Mother's grave. Yes, he had changed—he was dressed in a man's clothes now—but he was still a Unaka and remained ignorant of the good manners practiced in the Cherokee world. Besides, he was like a nosy raccoon, and he always came for something and never observed the Cherokee custom that says you should give something back. I wondered what he would soon be demanding of us.

Beloved Mother, though, had liked Jonathan. I heard her words in my head. *You will not talk to him in a scolding voice, Dancing Leaf,* she had told me more than once. *Why are you so annoyed? True, he has the rough manners of the Unaka, but he is a good boy. Perhaps he is your thunder being,* she had suggested with one eyebrow arched. *You must pay attention to what you can learn from him.*

A thunder being, I knew from Cherokee stories, is a person the Creator has put in your pathway. "A thunder being will often be the very opposite of you," Beloved Mother was fond of saying. "He is there to teach you a lesson. We learn how to live life more fully and how to think more fairly when we learn to live with a thunder being. I myself had many struggles with Dragging Canoe."

Dragging Canoe was Beloved Mother's cousin and good friend when they were children. But when they were older and the white man began to take the Cherokee lands, Dragging Canoe broke with the counsel of older chiefs and spent his days striking terror in the hearts of the white villages as chief warrior of the Chickamauga. Beloved Mother, meanwhile, married a white man and counseled her people to live at peace with the white world.

"Uh, Dancing Leaf. . . ."

I realized then that Jonathan had been talking to me but I had not been listening.

"I was saying I'm sorry, Dancing Leaf. Mother says I have a bad habit of spouting off whatever comes into my head."

"Perhaps you should think before you talk," I said evenly.

"Yes, you're right about that, Dancing Leaf."

My heart softened for a moment at this confession, but then Jonathan took his comb from his pocket and ran it through his whiskers. He also removed his hat and combed his hair. He had already done this twice during our ride. No doubt, he thought I would admire his long, golden locks, but his actions only irritated me. I said nothing, though, not wanting to take on his own rude manners. But again I wished I had not consented to take him to the grave.

We rode for a while in silence until Jonathan said, "Dancing Leaf, I've got something to tell you."

Dark clouds immediately gathered in my mind. Soon he would tell me this "something," and then he would also *ask* for something.

"You know I was in Chattanooga most of last year visiting Uncle Edgar," he began. "Well, Uncle Edgar's a minister, a man of God. When I was with him, I got the calling and now I know what I'm going to do with my life."

"Calling?" I asked. "What is a calling?"

"You know—a calling from the Lord. Like Samuel in the Old Testament. He heard the Lord's voice and knew he was to be a man of God. Or Paul in the New Testament. God struck him with blindness on the road to Damascus. For three days he was blind, then he heard the voice of the Lord telling him that he was to give up his previous life and become a true man of God. Well, I got my calling, too, and I'm going to be a preacher."

"So a calling is like a vision," I mused. "In past times Cherokee braves went on a vision quest, asking the Great Spirit to reveal their path in life."

"A vision, huh? Well, this is more like something you hear. The Lord told me he wanted me to be a minister—only he didn't really say it out loud—he said it to my heart, see. But I heard it just the same, and now I know."

I thought of the ministers who sometimes visited our school at Spring Place and preached on Sundays. I liked the preachers; they were kind to us and cared about us, but I did not always like what they said. They scared the little ones with their talk about hell and burning in fire, and sometimes they scared me. "How will you do this—be a minister?" I asked Jonathan.

"Well, I'll set up a church around here, and all of the white people will come on Sundays, and your people can come too. You could help. You could translate for the Cherokee who don't understand English."

"And where will this church be? Your white men will build it?"

"I was thinking we could use the old inn at first, until we get an established congregation, at least. Then maybe we'll want to build a new one."

I pulled the reins, and Red Sky came to a stop. "Old inn?" I asked. "What old inn?"

Jonathan's horse had taken a few more steps before stopping, so he had to turn around. After a dry cough he replied, "Well, yours, actually."

So. It was now only a small matter of letting him use our property for his purpose. I raised my eyes to Galunlati, silently imploring Beloved Mother to listen. *See?* my thoughts called out to her. *This Unaka is always looking for something from us.*

I turned my torso and strained to see if the inn was still visible in the distance, but it wasn't. I nudged Red Sky forward and thought about the inn. In earlier days, before Beloved Mother needed a walking stick, she and Long Fellow operated a lodge close to Woman Killer's Creek. Beloved Mother and I also lived there in a small bedroom in the top of the inn. But in later years—when she weakened with age and I was gone during the winter months, attending the mission school—we closed the inn and lived instead with Long Fellow in his cabin. I counted the years back and decided that five years had passed since the inn operated. When Five Killer moved nearby and built his own cabin, I thought perhaps he would resume the running of the inn, but so far he had not taken action.

"Five Killer will be opening the inn again," I said, as if the matter had been decided. "He will want it for a place of business; it could not be a place for white man's religion."

Perhaps my statement was not a complete truth, but I knew that neither Five Killer nor Long Fellow would allow such a church to be built. Besides, if I hadn't said that, Jonathan would be like a pesky mosquito, bothering us all summer.

We tied the horses to a low branch of the giant oak tree that grew beside the creek. Then we set out on foot to make the climb. The hill was steep, and the path I had worn in the fall was now barely visible. I felt pangs of guilt seeing the new growth; I should have come more days during the spring. At the top of the hill we walked toward the pile of stones that marked Beloved Mother's grave.

"Why all the stones?" Jonathan asked. "They don't brighten up the place or make it beautiful the way flowers do."

"It is the custom of our people that everyone places a stone on the grave. Tomorrow your flowers will be wilted, brown, and ugly. These stones will last forever, and no animal will be able to dig up the grave."

"You need a marker," Jonathan said. "You know—a stone or a wooden cross with her name on it." He took his flowers and wedged the stems under the rocks. "I could make one," he offered. "What should it say? Nancy Ward? Isn't that her Christian name?"

"Her name is Nanyehi," I said softly.

"Nun-ya-hey," he replied awkwardly, each syllable exploding from his lips.

"Nanyehi," I repeated, "like the sound of the summer breeze whispering through the pine forest."

"What does it mean?"

"It is a name for the spirit people who live around us and come to the rescue of the Cherokee in times of trouble."

"What about 'Beloved Mother'? Isn't that what you and other people call her? Isn't that a title of some sort?"

"Ghigau," I replied, using the Cherokee word for her title. "It means beloved woman, which is a rank of honor in our tribe."

"Sort of like queen or princess?" he asked.

"Well, it is as important as the title of queen or princess, but it is different. A beloved woman earns her rank. Beloved Mother fought in the Battle of Taliwa alongside her husband. When he died in battle, she took up his tomahawk and gun and gave the rallying cry to the other warriors. Instead of retreating, the Cherokee warriors pressed forward and defeated the Creeks."

"Imagine that," Jonathan said, crossing his arms and leaning back.

"She did many brave things. She sat with the chiefs at council meetings; she prepared the black drink for warriors going to battle; she offered prayers to the sacred fire during special ceremonies; often she saw visions that helped to guide her people."

He shook his head thoughtfully. "I just can't imagine little Granny Ward doing all that."

Once again my eyes turned upward as I implored Beloved Mother's spirit. *Did you hear him?* my mind screamed to the skies. *He called you "little Granny Ward."*

"Let us go," I said impatiently. "I have to work in the garden today, and there is much to do."

"Just a second." He reached into his bag and pulled out his Bible. "I want to read a passage over the grave."

"The minister from Brainerd has already said the prayer of the Good Shepherd."

"I'll read a different passage," he persisted.

"I'll wait at the bottom," I said impatiently. I wanted to tell him not to read a passage at all, but in my mind I saw Beloved Mother's frown and heard her scolding words from years past: *Yes, the Unakas are sometimes rude, but we are not to return their words or actions. We must learn how to live and work with them, for they are a powerful people.*

Slowly I descended the hill, turning my feet sideways and leaning back to keep my balance. Twice my moccasins slipped and I caught myself with outstretched hands before I went tumbling down. I watched as Jonathan descended. With his heavy boots, his steps were surer. When he reached the bottom, once again he removed his comb and pulled it through his hair—with difficulty now because it had tangled from the gusting wind on top of the hill.

I could not stand to watch and instead looked below to our farm in the distance. The straight rows of corn had begun their stretch skyward. Our cow, Rosie, was grazing in the fenced pasture. The barn appeared sturdy and well kept. Any stranger coming along might think it a Unaka farm. Many Cherokee families lived as we did on such farms. Cherokee towns, with huts surrounding the council house and scattered fields, still existed in the mountain regions, but they were few.

We untied our horses and led them to the creek and sat while they lapped at the water. Then Jonathan made known the second purpose for his visit.

"Say, Dancing Leaf, do you have any of the plant medicine that Granny—I mean Mrs. Ward—gave us for Grandfather's rheumatism. And how about that yellow stuff she gave me for that coon bite. Ma used that for all the kids' cuts and scrapes, and she swears it's the best thing for bringing the swelling down or for bringing a boil to a head."

"Well," I began slowly, trying to think of how I could escape giving him our medicine, "our supplies have dwindled since Beloved Mother's death. I do not keep up with the plants the way she did."

"How about if we just pick some up out here?" His arms made a sweeping gesture that included tree and sky and stream and meadow.

I sighed. The tassel flower for poultices grew along the road across from the pine thicket, and the fern that relieves rheumatism lived beside this very stream. My eyes searched forward and backward as the horses drank, and yes, I did see such a patch of fern. I looked up to Jonathan, who was watching me carefully. I did not think it wise to disclose Cherokee plant knowledge to a Unaka—Long Fellow always warned Beloved Mother against this—but then I remembered she had chided him, saying that the plant world existed for the benefit of all creation and not just the red man. And if I showed the plants to Jonathan, then he could gather them himself in the future and not be bothering me. I looked at the fern plant and back to him.

"That," I said pointing to the fuzzy leaves only a few horses' heads away, "is the plant we use to draw out the rheumatism. The fuzzy one—the fern."

He leapt up before I could gather my blue skirt around me, and in three strides he reached the fern and began pulling it with both hands. "I've got it," he called back to me. "You don't have to get muddy."

"Stop! Stop!" I yelled the words so loudly that the horses quit drinking and stumbled backwards several steps. "Do not touch any more plants," I commanded as I hurried to the place he was standing. My foot slipped, and the edge of my skirt dangled in the mud. I grabbed Jonathan's arm to steady myself and then began shaking it in anger when I saw how he had ravaged the plant from the ground. "You cannot remove a plant from his home in the earth without asking him for the favor!" I said sharply.

I held out my hands, and he put the bruised plants into them. Then I bent down and tried to reattach them to the damp earth, patting them gently.

"You must begin slowly, respectfully," I said as I straightened to face him again. "You ask the plant if he is willing to help with your intentions."

"Dancing Leaf," Jonathan replied with a smirk, "there's no need to get in a pucker. Besides, you don't need to talk to plants. They don't have brains or souls. God put them on this earth for us to use. You wouldn't ask a deer if he minded if you shot him, now would you?"

"Yes," I replied. I took a kernel of corn from my medicine pouch and bent down again and placed it on the wounded ferns. "I am sorry, little plant, that we have disturbed you. Please do not be angry with us. This one is a Unaka and has not been taught properly, and I was not fast enough. Please accept my gift of corn as a peace offering."

"You mean to tell me that you do ask permission of the deer?" he asked incredulously.

"Yes." I placed three more kernels of corn on the fern plants. "And another matter," I added as I rose again. "You must never take the first plant you see, or the second or the third. Only the fourth plant may be taken, and every fourth plant after that."

I bent over and washed my hands in the running stream and stood and dried them on my skirt. "When we leave," I continued, "we thank the plant kingdom and always leave an offering, perhaps a few kernels of corn or a pinch of tobacco."

But Jonathan was not listening and instead was holding up his black book. "It says in here that God created man to have dominion over the plants and animals."

"What does *dominion* mean?"

"It means we rule them."

"I think it means we are to be their caretakers," I countered. "We must leave this place now, for you have offended the plant kingdom."

"You can't offend a plant, Dancing Leaf!" He sat down on a mossy spot and began paging through his book.

I lowered myself to the ground then, too, for it seemed we had much more to discuss. "Plants are our good friends," I explained. "They have been our friends since the time the animal kingdom became angry with men. We were killing too many animals, and also there were so many of us, we were crowding them out. So animals sent us diseases. The plants felt sorry for us and held council. They decided for every illness the animals inflicted, they would provide a remedy in the plant world."

"Well, Dancing Leaf, that is a silly story. The book of Genesis says that God made the heavens and the earth and everything that dwells upon it. And the final thing he made was man, and man is the smartest; he's the only one with brains and soul and spirit. It says so in here," he said, shaking his Bible at me.

"We are all descended from the spirit world," I informed him as I rose again. "You are right—the plants did come first. Then the birds and animals, and finally the humans. We are younger than them, and we have much to learn from them. From plants we learn about taking care of health, and from animals about how to survive in this world, and from birds we learn about spirit freedom."

I grabbed the reins of Red Sky. I spoke sharply to Jonathan as I mounted. "It is time to leave. You are, no doubt, anxious to return to your home, and I have much to do also."

"Well, I hate to go home without any of the remedy," he argued. "Grandpa's rheumatism is bad, and Henry has a cut on his hand where he got hold of Ma's kitchen knife."

I could turn down this rude Unaka but not a poor, crying baby or a weak old man. "Very well," I said. "I will see what we have in the cabin."

"One more thing," Jonathan persisted.

I looked skyward again. What could be his next request?

"Do you have a pair of scissors?" he asked. "I've been wanting to cut my hair, and Ma lent our scissors to Aunt Cora."

"Ah, yes, we do have scissors. And I could cut your hair," I said with a smile. "But first you will have to listen to the story of the possum with the beautiful tail."

"Possums don't have beautiful tails," he argued.

"They once did," I answered.

When we reached the cabin, it was empty. I assumed Long Fellow had gone to Five Killer's cabin and taken Chera with him. I found the two remedies in the cupboard. I sprinkled some from each onto squares of muslin cloth and then bound them up with thin strands of rope. Jonathan put them into his satchel and hurried out. He did not ask again about the haircut.

I was exhausted because spending time with a thunder being is very tiring. I thought I would lie down and take a nap, but I heard a dog barking and it was not Chera's bark. It sounded like Blackie.

I started up the hill to Five Killer's and saw Blackie's head appear from under the porch. Blue Lake's horse was standing nearby, tied to the tree.

THE UKTENA

The Uktena was a monstrous snake as large as a tree trunk. He had a horn on his head, and behind the horn was a bright, blazing crystal. The scales on his body sparkled like fire. His body was so hard that arrows, spears, and bullets could not penetrate it. Spots of color ran from his nose to his tail. The seventh spot from his head was his only vulnerable spot, for under this spot was his heart. The Uktena was a dangerous snake, and many warriors tried to kill him. They especially wanted the crystal he carried on his head, for the possessor of this crystal would have great powers.

The great warrior Aganunitsi searched the dark passages of the Smoky Mountains where the great serpent was known to lie in wait for his unsuspecting victims. When Aganunitsi reached Gahuti Mountain, he found the Uktena asleep. Quickly he dug a trench below the Uktena and filled it with fire. Then Aganunitsi shot the Uktena with an arrow that pierced the seventh spot, through to his heart.

The great snake rose and charged after him but soon rolled over dead from the arrow. In his death struggle, however, he spit out rivers of poison that rolled down the mountainside. The poison was stopped by the circle of fire. Blood, too, ran from the monster and soon filled up the trench and became a stream. The monster rolled down the mountainside, toppling tree after tree.

Aganunitsi called in all of the birds of the bird clan, and they devoured the monster until nothing was left but his carcass and a sparkling light—the sacred crystal. Aganunitsi quickly wrapped it and took it with him. From that time on, he was the greatest medicine man of the tribe.

Chapter 3

Blue Lake came slowly down the hill from Five Killer's cabin. Chera trotted beside him. He was walking easily as if he had no place special to go. Of course, I wondered why he was here, but I did not let myself dwell on reasons. Instead, I tossed my braids behind my back and crossed my arms, pulling them in close as I stood tall.

"Hello, Dancing Leaf," he began as he stopped in front of me.

I pressed my hand on my heart to steady the beat, for when Blue Lake said my name, his voice touched a sacred place, and everything inside of me trembled in response. I looked into his eyes—they were so round, so blue, so true. They never skittered about when he talked; they never stared off into the distance when I spoke to him; always they were calm and sure.

He placed his hands on my arms and gently pushed me toward the steps. "Let us sit down, here on the porch, and talk."

I let myself be seated, and he sat beside me, and although my heart was fluttering like a trapped bird, still I kept my arms folded and my back straight.

"I had to come back for Blackie," he said. "The rope broke when I was some five miles out. Blackie turned around and ran like a panther, never looking back. I couldn't catch him."

"Where is he now?" I asked.

"Hiding under Five Killer's porch." He grinned when he said that, and I thought he didn't seem to mind returning so much.

"And now what will you do?"

"Tomorrow we leave with a stronger rope."

"Yes, that would be wise."

"Five Killer says we should talk about this . . . about my leaving. I wanted to, but you . . . you've seemed so angry, I was afraid."

I pulled myself in tighter and refused to look at him. I did not like that he said I was angry.

"Part of me wants to go," he continued. "It will be a great adventure to travel and see a big city. It will be good to see my father and his family, and perhaps I will inherit land and other things."

"Yes, that would be good."

"But part of me doesn't want to go." He tugged at my arm, loosening my grip, and slid his hand into mine. "I will miss you."

Still my back and neck were in a straight line, and my nose pointed forward. I took a deep breath, though, and my shoulders relaxed. I began picking at the weed stickers that had attached to my skirt. One of them was so sharp, it cut my finger. A drop of blood spilled out, and I quickly put the finger to my mouth.

"Will you miss me?" he asked.

I did not look at him as I answered. "I would miss you if you were coming back, but if you aren't returning, then you will have to be like the life that I once had long ago before I was brought to live with Beloved Mother. That life is gone from me. I cannot remember it."

"I thought that's what you would say." He let my hand slip from his, and he leaned forward, resting his chin in his cupped palms. We sat in silence for a few minutes, then he turned to me and said in a voice of softened anger, "Dancing Leaf, I will miss you either way. I will think of you every day. I will remember the evenings we waded the stream and speared catfish. I will remember how we sat on the rock as the sun set, telling stories of our early days. I will think of your blue skirt and the ribbons in your braids. I will see your deerskin box where you keep your writing. When the leaves begin to fall, I will remember the day you and Chera chased them in the wind."

He stood then and faced me and took both of my hands in his own. "I will think of you milking the cow and gathering eggs in your basket and riding on the dappled horse. I will never forget you. But I don't know if I will come back; I just don't know."

"I want you to come back." The words tumbled out and surprised me as much as they did Blue Lake. It did not seem a wise thing to say. "I don't have a family," I added, realizing that this was the first time I had given words to this thought. "Not since Beloved Mother died."

"But you do! You have Long Fellow and Five Killer. And there are always Beloved Mother's daughters, Betsy and Catherine, who do not live far away. I am the one without a family."

"I love Long Fellow and Five Killer, but I still don't feel like this is my family. And they are not comfortable either. Oftentimes I wonder if they would prefer that I live with Betsy or Catherine, but those two have their own children and grandchildren."

"It has been the same with me. Five Killer has been good to me, but I do not think of him as my father, and he does not think of me as a son either."

"But now you have a family. You have your father, and even when he dies there will be other relatives you will meet . . . aunts and uncles." But as I said the words, I realized that Blue Lake must feel as I did—alone.

"I have something for you," he announced, abruptly changing the subject. He reached into his pocket and took out a small object wrapped in blue cloth. He put it in my hand and closed my fingers around it.

Slowly my fingers raised, one by one, and then with my other hand I unwrapped the blue cloth, revealing a crystal—a clear, quartz crystal, not too large to be worn around the neck, not so small as to be lost easily. "A crystal?" My voice was a whisper. "A crystal is a sacred stone." In the old days, only priests were allowed to have them. Everyone knew they were powerful medicine, and they were always used in special ceremonies. "Where did you get it?"

"It belonged to my mother, and before that it belonged to her mother, and before that it belonged to her father, who was a white peace chief in Nikwasi before the village was destroyed in the war with the whites."

"Are you sure you want to part with this?"

He sat down beside me again, and his arm went around my waist. I no longer sat stiff and tall. "I cannot take it with me," he said. "It belongs to the Cherokee world, and where I am going is not the Cherokee world. You are right. The crystal is something sacred that needs to be protected and treasured. Mother often prayed with it cupped in her palms. Besides, if you take the crystal, then I know you can never forget me either."

I could say nothing, for I felt a large knot in my throat, and streams of tears flowed from my eyes.

Blue Lake sighed and took my hand in his again. "Dancing Leaf, you are sad. That is one reason I leave. We have been together every day for a year now, and always you are sad."

"But that is because Beloved Mother died."

"Maybe in part, but there is something more. It is a larger sadness that leaves a hole in your center; something needs to fill this sadness, and I don't think I can do it. Maybe when I'm gone, you will come to understand this sadness and learn how to fill the empty hole."

"Have I made you sad, too?" Even as I asked the question, I knew I sounded like a child of six and not a young woman of sixteen years. "I did not mean to make you sad."

"When you are sad, I am sad, but I am glad we have been together."

Then I was like a thunderstorm breaking loose, no longer content to splatter small droplets. Torrents of tears flowed down my cheeks, and my whole body shook. Blue Lake drew me in, and I cried on his shoulder. I knew my tears were wetting his shirt, but I could not help myself. Still, I scolded myself as I cried, and I wondered how I could be two completely different people.

Just that morning I had been proud and strong with Jonathan. But with Blue Lake things were so different. We never argued, even when I wanted to, and I often felt like a helpless newborn around him. No wonder he looked forward to a trip that would take him far away. Perhaps in Virginia he would meet a pretty Unaka girl who would make him laugh and dance and sing. My thoughts brought more tears, but I did not speak of these fears with Blue Lake.

Finally he stood and pulled me up with him. "Enough crying," he said. "We have this evening together, and we can spend it happily. I want to remember you laughing and dancing."

Five Killer came down to tell us "the old ones" were going into town.

Raven wished to buy material for skirts and shirts, and Long Fellow would buy coffee and tobacco. So Blue Lake and I went to the stream, where we speared a catfish and a frog for supper. We cooked them outside and ate on a blanket by the flowing water. We waded down the stream to the place where raspberries grow and picked a basketful, eating as many as we placed in the basket. We raced back to the cabin, and Blue Lake won, even though I insisted he start behind me at the edge of the pine trees.

When the sun had set on the other side of the hill, we sat on my rock, two people folded together like one—my back leaning against his chest, his arms around my legs—and we watched the blue and red glowing embers of clouds that streaked across the sky until they slipped behind the darkness of the distant ridge.

When the others came by on the wagon, we jumped on the back and rode home with them. Everyone slept together in Long Fellow's cabin that night instead of Five Killer and Raven going to their own. It was a warm night that seemed to slowly melt away.

And then it was morning, and we stood on the porch again, and Blue Lake once more rode off with Blackie and the rope.

"Did he get a stronger rope?" I asked Five Killer. "That looks like the same one he used yesterday. Blackie will break it again."

"He trailed the Unaka boy back, not Blackie," Five Killer said.

"The Unaka boy? Jonathan?" Five Killer's words surprised me. "Jonathan always comes to ask for something, but surely Blue Lake knows he would not steal from us."

"He was not worried about the things he might take," Five Killer answered. "He was afraid he would steal the heart of a Cherokee maiden."

My eyes grew wide and round like the eyes of the owl. It took a few moments for the meaning of his words to go from my head to my heart, and then I felt a warm glow. Perhaps Five Killer was right. Maybe Blue Lake had been jealous that Jonathan was with me. My fingers caressed the crystal in my waist pouch. This new idea required more thought.

Five Killer broke into my reverie. "What did the Unaka want?"

"I almost forgot. He thinks to be a minister now, a man of God. He wants to use our inn for Sunday meetings. I am supposed to ask you about it. He says the white people and the Cherokee will both come."

Five Killer snorted like a horse protesting a bridle.

"He said he has already spoken to the Indian agent about it," I continued, "and he has written to several of our chiefs to see if the idea finds favor with them."

"Well, I, too, have been thinking of the inn. Perhaps we should reopen it. We can sell and trade goods both with whites and Indians. We will open the rooms again for travelers. Raven has often urged me to do so."

"Yes, I like the idea too," I agreed, remembering the days filled with traveling people and traders with wagons of bright goods. The scents of cooking food, coffee, and pipe tobacco were always with us, and the evenings were filled with stories and long talks.

"Jonathan will have to build his own meeting place," Five Killer declared. "Our inn will be a place of business. This is what we will tell him."

But in the next week, Five Killer went on a hunt with Corn Walker, an old friend who came to visit, and was gone for three days. When he returned, I heard no talk of working on the inn.

"Five Killer has never been one to enjoy farming or business," Long Fellow reminded me. "He has always had the spirit of the warrior and the hunter. In his younger days he fought with Dragging Canoe."

What Long Fellow said was true. Five Killer had moved back to the home of his family only a few years ago, when open conflict with the white world had finally ceased. Raven had been living with him for this past year, and we all referred to her as his wife, although we did not know if they had had a formal ceremony.

Raven was some years younger than Five Killer, and she was a beautiful woman. She was tall and stately like the live oak trees growing alongside the river, but she had roundness in the places that men like to see it. Her face had the smoothness, the color, and the contour of the acorn. Her long, black hair had the sheen of raven feathers and hung nearly to her waist. In the hot summer months, she plaited it and wound it around her head. She was past the age of bearing children but still had no gray hairs—although I suspected she used the bark of walnut root, for one day I saw several silver strands, and the next day there were none. When she walked in town, Five Killer walked close to her, for men often turned to stare at her.

Raven loved to work with cloth. After Five Killer purchased a spinning wheel, she often spun her own. Other times she bought it in parcels from traders or from the store in town. She sewed shirts and breeches for Five Killer, Long Fellow, and even Blue Lake. She made skirts and dresses for herself and for her daughter who lived in Coosa Town. She had never made anything for me, however, and I did not ask her, even though both my blue skirt and my brown one were old and worn. When I held them up, I could see light shining through. I took care not to scrub them when I washed them in the stream. Raven also made belts and mats and blankets that she often traded for other things.

So the work of the farm was left to Long Fellow and me, and Long Fellow could not work in the hot sun as he used to. He required naps in the afternoon, and he had never learned to milk the cow. I was the one, then, who tended the garden, pulling weeds and checking the progress of vegetables. We grew corn, beans, squash, and potatoes. Pumpkin, too, which would not be ripe till fall. The early corn had already ripened. I roasted some of it for daily meals and spent many hours soaking, pounding, and sifting the rest for bread and biscuits. We ate some of the beans likewise each evening, and the others I strung and dried in the storage house. I gathered and dried berries also for the winter months. And there was the cow to milk and the eggs to gather. I became angry that Blue Lake had left when so much work needed to be done.

I worried, too, as everyone did, about the dryness of the summer. Many of the vines in the garden had withered and turned brown. The beans were small, and the potatoes were long and thin, not plump and full as they had been last year. The heat and the dry weather had made the forest creatures bolder, and they raided our garden each evening. Chera and I slept on the porch so she could keep watch. Every night I woke to her howls and heard her scurrying after some creature, and in the morning I saw tracks of rabbits and raccoons and possums. I was glad Blue Lake had not taken her, and now I could see the bulge of her belly, but still she guarded well our patch of garden.

But it was not Chera's scampering alone that kept me from a restful sleep. Bad dreams were upon me for the third time in my life. The first time they occurred was after the Unakas burned and destroyed the village of my first home. Then after Beloved Mother died last fall, again I could not sleep for many nights, and when I did, I often awoke crying and trembling. And now I was having bad dreams again. Perhaps the heat and the many awakenings throughout the night disturbed my sleep. I did not want to think Blue Lake's departure had caused such problems.

These dreams were different from the dreams of earlier years, though. Before, my dreams were dark and full of shadows, and I could seldom remember them. But this time the dreams were filled with the creatures of Cherokee legend, and the events seemed so real that my mind dwelled on them over and over during the day. I dreamed the large snake Uktena appeared to me, and on his head was a crystal. But it was not the magic crystal; it was the crystal that Blue Lake had given to me. I was afraid to reach out and take it, and when I looked into the Uktena's eyes I saw that they were blue. I dreamed of Spearfinger, the stone-covered monster woman who lures small children. She told me I was too large for her now, and if I would just give her my liver, she would leave me alone.

I dreamed a dream that started out a happy dream. I was walking in the woods and knocked on a cabin door, and my first mother answered. I knew this woman was my first mother because she called me by my old name, the name I had before Beloved Mother adopted me. "Well, come in, Falling Leaf," she said. "We have been looking for you for a long time." So I went into the cabin, where I was greeted by my father, too. The two of them made a fine meal of venison stew and corn bread, which we shared. I fell asleep on a pallet they fixed for me, but I awoke that night to see them roasting something in the fire, and when I looked, I knew it was the heart of a human. I knew then that they were not my parents; they were raven-mockers—evil spirit people who can transform into other shapes and bodies and steal the hearts of dying people. With each heart they eat, they add as many years to their life as the victim would have had left if he had lived his full life. In terror, I watched them devour the heart. I could not move and knew I would be their next victim.

All of these dreams I had over and over, but the one I hated most was the one with Stone Man. Stone Man traveled with a cane made of bright, shining rock. This cane was a magic cane and would lead him to the place where a man was hunting or a woman was gathering berries. I was hiding in the dream. And I was hiding in the same bush where I hid when I was a small child and my mother sent me to the river to hide from the soldiers burning our village. The Stone Man came toward me with his shining cane. I knew he saw me, so I stood. "I am no longer a child!" I yelled as loudly as I could. "I am now a young woman of child-bearing age!" Only a young woman could kill Stone Man, and she could kill him easily with one look. And so he ran away, but he looked back once, and when he did, I saw that he had the face of Blue Lake, and then I was sad because I knew it had not been Stone Man after all, but only Blue Lake, and I had scared him away.

My dreams were disturbing to Long Fellow. Often I awoke screaming or yelling loud words, and he would shake me until I returned to the waking world. "Yes, Dancing Leaf," he assured me after the last dream, "you are now a woman. You do not need to be afraid of Stone Man or anyone else. Now go to sleep and have good dreams."

I knew he counseled with Five Killer after that evening, because Five Killer came to me and said, "These dreams are not good. I have thought to send for Lame Deer, the adawehi, but Raven tells me a well-respected adawehi lives in Coosa Town, where her daughter remains, and that he is very skilled with dispelling bad dreams. She will go with you and see that you are well attended."

I did not like this idea—for many reasons—although I did not tell them to Five Killer. "My dreams are not so bad," I insisted. "I am sure I can make them stop. Besides, you should send Long Fellow to the adawehi for his snoring, because many nights I fear his rumblings will shake the walls of the cabin down."

Five Killer laughed. "Yes, you are right about Long Fellow's snoring. But I am worried about you, Dancing Leaf. Anyone can see that you are not happy. You go about doing your work during the day, but you do not skip or smile or sing or laugh anymore. We must try to make you happy again."

Tears filled my eyes, and I turned my head so he would not see.

"Besides," he continued, "Long Fellow says I will have to come and sleep in the cabin with you if you do not quit these dreams, and he will sleep in my cabin. He is an old man and needs his sleep."

As I looked at Five Killer, I noticed the deep lines on his face. They reminded me of the cracked earth that forms in dry creek beds. He still had many hairs on his head, but they were the color of the white ashes left from an evening fire. I thought to tell him that he was an old man, too, who needed his sleep, but I could not tease the way he did, and I was afraid I would offend him.

"Will you take me to Coosa Town?" I asked.

He coughed first and then folded his arms to his chest and rubbed his toe against his shin before he answered. "Someone needs to stay here with Long Fellow, and I don't think it could be Raven. Besides, she misses her daughter and has been searching for a reason to visit her."

I thought as much but did not say anything.

"It is good of her to want to take you," he added. "You must treat her well and take care of her."

I was annoyed but still said nothing, as I did not wish to annoy Five Killer. I knew he saw only beauty when he looked at Raven.

THE BEAR PEOPLE

There was a boy who loved to go into the woods every day. He would leave at daybreak, stay out all day, and come home after the evening meal. His parents scolded him and tried to persuade him to spend time with them, but it did no good. One day they noticed hair growing all over his body, and this worried them.

"What are you doing anyway?" they demanded.

"Plenty of food exists out there, and I don't have to work for it or worry about it. I even like the food better. Besides, I am starting to look different and soon will not be able to live here. I will live in the woods all of the time and will not come back. You can come, too, but first you must fast for seven days."

The parents talked it over with the head men of the town and persuaded them that this might be a better way to live. So they all fasted for seven days, and when the time was up, the entire town went with the family to the woods. The people in the neighboring towns heard of this and were sorry to lose their friends and sent messengers to see if they might be called back. But already the people of the woods were changing, for they had not eaten human food for seven days. The townsmen who now lived in the woods would not come back but offered this message to their friends:

"We are going to a place with abundant food, and now we are a different people. We will be called 'bear.' Now when you become hungry, you may come into the woods and call us and we will come to give you our own flesh. Do not be afraid to kill us, for we will live always."

They taught the messengers the song to call the bear. And so it is that each morning the bear hunter starts out by fasting and singing the bear song.

Chapter 4

Chera was another reason I did not want to leave. I saw the bulge on both sides of her stomach when she stood before me. Any day now she would have puppies. Already she had been abandoned by Blue Lake.

"I don't think she should be outside at night anymore," I informed Long Fellow.

"She will stay inside if she wants, Dancing Leaf," he said in an easy manner. "Animals know what they can and cannot do, better than humans."

"But this is her first litter, so she does not know, and she has no mother to teach her."

Long Fellow smiled. "The Creator puts inside each animal's mind the way of life, and so they are not as dependent on their parents as we are. Besides, you will probably be gone for only three or four days."

I consoled myself with that thought, but the matter of caring for Long Fellow remained.

"You must see that Long Fellow drinks comfrey tea before he retires every evening," I instructed Five Killer. "And if he snores, you must roll him on his side. When he lies on his back, his breath comes unevenly, and it sounds like wind trying to enter through a crack in the wall. That is not good; he needs his rest. Also, try to persuade him to use a walking stick, at least when no one else is around. He is too stubborn to use it if he thinks anyone will see him."

"Ah, Dancing Leaf, you will make a fine wife and mother," Five Killer replied.

"I will?" Though his words were meant to tease me, I wanted to know if truth existed in them. I feared just the opposite—that I would not know what to do when the time came to be a wife and mother.

"Yes, it is true," he affirmed. He stepped behind me and swept his arms around my shoulders, pulling me in close. "Your only problems are you worry too much and have bad dreams. Still . . . you have a pure and loving heart."

"I do?" I wrestled from his grip, and my eyes jumped to his, searching the truth.

"Yes," he replied; his eyes were still dancing, but he nodded firmly and his arms circled me again.

"Do not forget to milk the cow," I warned, "or she will swell and become infected. That is how the Youngs' cow died."

Five Killer made a face. He did not like cows or milk from cows and would not drink it.

Raven decided we should hitch Red Sky, the dappled horse, to the wagon and ride in this manner to the settlement of Coosa Town. This I did not want to do. "Raven, you have said yourself we travel over a mountainous country. The horse alone will have difficulty maneuvering the passes. We may not be able to get the wagon through."

"I have been there many times," Raven informed me. "Five Killer had no problem before, and you will not either."

Ah, so I would be the one holding the reins and trying to get us through the difficult places. At least the path would not be a slippery one, I reasoned, and for a moment I was glad we had had so little rain.

Perhaps Raven was afraid to ride on the back of a horse, I considered, as I had never seen her do this before. But when it came time to depart, and Five Killer began carrying bundles out, then I knew why we needed the wagon. He brought out parcels of cloth to make clothes, several iron pots because the villagers in Coosa Town still used clay ones, and soft blankets for the cold nights of mountain air for Raven's grandbabies—the deer hides her daughter used were much too hard for a baby's skin. He also carried out belts and sashes, for gifts to friends, along with other bundles of which I could only guess.

So we loaded up the wagon and waved farewell to Five Killer, Long Fellow, and Chera, all standing on the porch. I was proud of Chera, who did not whimper or whine as we left, but barked only once when I called out to her. I knew then she had understood my talk with her earlier in the morning. I had explained that I must travel to the adawehi, who would give me treatment for bad dreams. I reminded her that her puppies would be in this world any day now and that she must rest; I told her to take care of them well if she had them before I returned. In a matter of a few days, I promised, I would be with her again.

We rode in silence over the flat meadows, the wagon wheels churning small dust clouds. When we entered the hill country, Raven asked, "Did you bring a rifle?" She glanced uneasily toward the dense woods on either side.

"I have no rifle," I answered.

"But Long Fellow does and Five Killer also," she said with irritation. "We may need a rifle."

My mind formed the words *Well, then did you bring a rifle?* but I did not ask this, because Beloved Mother always frowned when I was disrespectful to an elder. Instead I replied, "We will not need a rifle."

My eyes squinted as I looked to the sun, whose rays now pierced the top of my head. I wished that we had left much earlier, but Raven always remained in bed until after the mists had risen from the hills. The sun, I feared, was scorching everything in her pathway as she made her daily trek across the sky. The grass of the meadows was already the color of winter hay; the flowers along the road were choked with dust, and the stems and vines withered. My head felt as if it were roasting on a spit, and streams of sweat poured down my face and arms. My eyes stung with each blink. At least Raven had a parasol that she raised over her head; I wished I had brought the bonnet that Beloved Mother had worn in the garden.

"Do not squint so," Raven lectured, "or you will offend the sun."

"Ah, yes," I answered because Raven was referring to the story about the mother sun who was angered because her earth children always frowned when they looked at her. "That is a story I haven't heard in a long time. I will have to write it on my paper and put it with the other stories."

Although I kept my own eyes fixed on the horse and road, I could tell Raven was studying me, as if she were measuring her next words. But she said nothing, so I ventured forward. "Why is it that in some of the stories the sun is a man and the moon a woman, and in others it is the other way around? Have you ever thought about that? What did your elders tell you?"

"I am sure they would have said, 'no matter,'" Raven answered. She paused for a moment, and I could see that her eyes traveled from the top of my head to my feet below. "Dancing Leaf, you waste too much time with your writing," she continued. "What good is it? You are a young woman now, and you must concern yourself with the business of learning to care for a man and children."

The reins dropped from my right hand, and I had to reach out to retrieve them. Raven's words were like a jolting rock underfoot. Of course, I knew she thought these things, but she had never given them utterance before.

"I say these things because you have no mother now," she continued, "and someone must help to prepare you for life ahead."

"Beloved Mother was pleased when I spent time writing words on paper," I reminded her.

"Well, she is not here, is she? And if you ask me, in her old age she was too easy with you. She should have demanded that you spend more time with women's work."

I held my breath then, for I wanted to remind Raven that in the last months of Beloved Mother's life, I had spent most of my time caring for her and for all of the other things in the household. And besides, the spirits above were surely frowning down on Raven now because she was speaking disrespectfully of a departed elder. But it was not my place to remind her of these things, so I held in my words.

She shifted her parasol to her other hand. "It is so hot!" she complained. "And my arms cannot continue holding this parasol." She looked at my arms for a moment, and I thought she might suggest that I use one hand to hold the parasol.

"It takes two arms to guide the reins," I said, "and already my arms are aching. I will hold the parasol, though, if you want to guide the reins." This I knew she would not do, and she ignored my question and simply sighed and frowned.

"Dancing Leaf," she began after a moment of silence, "I will try to say and do the things a mother would say and do for you—as much as I can. I have my own daughter and Five Killer also to care for. But you can see I try, for I am taking you to the adawehi, am I not?"

"Yes, we are traveling to the adawehi." Those were the words I said with my mouth. The words in my mind said, *No, it is I who take you to the village of Coosa Town to visit with your daughter.* Besides, I would have preferred being treated by Lame Deer, who lives only half a mile from us and who treated Beloved Mother for the crippling pain in her last days.

Raven shifted the parasol to her other arm and sighed a large sigh of frustration. "Your purpose in life at this time is to find a husband. Surely you must know this. Why are you not concerned?"

"I have many concerns," I answered.

"But this is the most important. I do not understand why you did not fix your attentions on Blue Lake. He is a fine Cherokee brave. Someone will be happy to be his wife. I have seen the two of you together, and I know he has feelings for you, but you did not attend to him as you should have."

Her scolding words normally caused my face to flush with anger, but the other words—*I know he has feelings for you*—caused my heart to dance. I wanted to ask her how she knew this, but instead I answered, "Blue Lake must find his path in life. I did not want to interfere and insist he stay with me."

"Every man must find his own path, but in every man's path is a woman. Blue Lake could have taken you with him."

This time my back came up straight, and I pulled the reins with a jerk. Red Sky turned to look at me, wondering if I truly wished to stop. I shook the reins to let her know to go on.

Raven's stabbing words pierced my heart. *Blue Lake could have taken you with him.* I had not allowed myself to dwell upon that thought until

43

this very moment, but now I could not escape it. Why hadn't Blue Lake asked me to go along? Oh, there were many reasons. He had his father and his white family to think of. And I am an Indian; perhaps they would not accept a full-blood. Or perhaps he was afraid I would not want to leave Long Fellow. But then Blue Lake's words echoed in my mind—*a sadness that leaves a hole in your center*—and I knew the truth: my unhappiness had driven Blue Lake away from me.

"Perhaps you should turn your attentions now to the Unaka boy, Jonathan," Raven continued. "He seems to like you, and— Do not look at me with an ugly face!"

I made my face smooth again; I had not realized I was making an ugly face, but the picture in my mind was an ugly picture.

"Jonathan is a fine boy," she went on. "He says he wishes to be a minister, so you can see he is a good man. Besides, Beloved Mother herself was married to a Unaka."

"Raven," I said, deciding it was time to talk of other things, "my arms are tired, and my shoulders ache. I cannot go on. Perhaps you would like to guide the horse."

"Well, you know that I cannot do that," she replied, tossing her head scornfully.

And so we rode on in silence for some time. Twice I climbed down from the wagon and led Red Sky through a narrow passageway with jagged rocks. We were traveling upward, and the air was cooler, but Red Sky pulled with head bent down, and her breath wheezed with the effort.

When the sun was just beginning her afternoon descent, we came to a flat place where grass grew along the bank of a stream. "We will stop here," I announced to Raven.

"But it cannot be that much farther," she protested. She stood and her eyes searched the distance.

"The horse must drink and rest, and we must eat," I insisted. So I led Red Sky to the stream, where she drank her fill, and then I tied the reins to a low branch of the tree. We spread the blanket on the grassy place, and we unwrapped bundles with strips of dried deer meat. I found the clay pot filled with strawberries and blackberries.

"You brought the corn bread?" I asked Raven.

She looked surprised and retorted, "You were supposed to bring the corn bread."

"But you said this morning you had made corn bread for our trip; you did not ask me to retrieve it, and I assumed you would bring it."

"I had many things to bring," she answered. "You only had yourself. You should have reminded me of the corn bread."

I remembered the small bag of wissactaw—parched corn meal—bundled with my clothes, and I retrieved it and put a small amount in our drinking cups, mixing it with water from the stream. We drank the thick mixture and ate all that we had, and still I was hungry. Raven was in no hurry now, for she had stretched out on the blanket in the cool shade of the trees above and seemed content to rest.

"I will wade down a bit and see what I can find." I hoped to discover a patch of berries or perhaps some watercress.

My eyes searched both sides of the narrow stream, but I saw no berries or watercress and determined that I should go just a little farther, when suddenly I was aware of noises that I had not heard before. The squirrels in the trees above barked noisily, and one of them ran to the end of the branch and scolded me. The birds were chattering frantically.

Red Sky whinnied and stomped the ground, and when I turned to look at her, I saw that she struggled to break free from the tree branch. A low growl drew my gaze to the shoreline. A black bear, standing upright like a man, pawed the air. Red Sky broke from the tree and galloped past me with the wagon behind, despite my protests. I did not have time to go after her, though, and I turned my attention to the bear, who was now roaring loudly.

Raven jumped to her feet with a piercing scream. My mind raced as fast as my feet, and I realized I would not have time to sing the bear song, reminding him of the friendship that existed between us. He took three steps toward her, and Raven backed into the water. He then dropped to four legs and charged. Raven floundered backwards a few more steps and fell into the water. She covered her face with her arms, just as the bear swiped forward. Drops of blood spurted into the air.

I yelled as loudly as I could and continued running toward them.

"I am coming, Bear! I am not afraid!" When he stopped and turned to stare at me, I bent down and picked up stones and threw them at him. "I am not afraid, Bear!" I yelled once more, and I threw another stone, which hit him on the nose.

He rose and once again roared, but when he stopped, we heard a slighter, echoing roar from the woods on the other side of the road. The bear turned to look, and my gaze followed his. A bear cub was standing on a rock, and when his mother fixed her eyes on him, he sat down.

"Ah, there is your baby, Mother Bear," I counseled softly. "You must go to him. We will pack up our things and leave, and then you can bring him down to the water."

She stared at me as if she were thinking about it, then turned and dropped to being a four-legged animal again and trotted toward her baby. She did not stop or look back, but simply grunted when she reached the rock, and the two of them disappeared into the woods.

Meanwhile Raven was moaning, and once the bear was gone, her moaning grew louder.

I ran to her. "Hush! The bear may come back. She may think you are threatening her."

I saw immediately, though, that the cuts on the arm were deep. The inner layers of pink flesh were visible where the skin parted. She had two gashes on her face, but they were not as deep as the ones on her arm. I reached for the medicine bag around my waist and was glad I had not left it in the wagon. I did not know where the wagon was, but I knew that I should attend to the wounds first. So I helped Raven hold her arm under the running water of the stream. Her arm shook with pain, and I tried to soothe her by telling her we would soon have it mended. I mixed the yellow root powder with droplets of water, making a paste that I dabbed on the inner flesh. Then I tore strips of cloth from my skirt and wrapped them around her arm so that the flesh came together. I dabbed more yellow paste on the cuts on her face, and then I led her to the blanket.

"Lie still," I commanded. "I must fetch Red Sky and the wagon."

She made no protest, as I feared she might. I waded down the stream and found the horse and wagon, but the wheel of the wagon was broken, and I did not have the tools to fix it. I unhitched the horse and loaded what I could onto her back and then led her back to the place where Raven lay.

"The wagon is broken; we can only take the horse. We will have to walk."

Raven sat up and looked about. "None of this would have happened if you had not insisted we stop to rest," she said bitterly.

I did not answer, nor did I offer to help her to her feet. I gathered our things, wrapped them in a cloth bundle to put on Red Sky's back, and then walked away, leaving Raven behind.

"You must wait," she protested. "I am injured and cannot travel easily."

So I stopped and waited until she reached my spot, and then we resumed walking slowly.

Raven was silent for several minutes, but then she voiced fears about her torn flesh. "Have you ever tended wounds before? If it is not done properly, there will be painful swelling, and the wounds will ooze a dangerous sap." She paused and looked at me. "I am told this sap can poison the body in less than a day."

"The root paste will do its work," I assured her.

"What about my face? Are the scratches deep there, too?" Her fingers lightly touched her face. "Did you bring a looking glass? I must see how deep they are. I do not want them to leave a scar."

"They are not as deep," I replied. "I think they will mend well, but you must keep your face still so that the skin is not stretched. I think it would be better if you did not talk."

"None of this would have happened if you had not insisted we stop to rest," she repeated.

The road was a constant climb, but it wound around the mountain so it was not so steep. Several times we paused for breath in places where we could see the valley below and the mountains that stretched above. I thought of the story that tells how the mountains were created when the great buzzard flapped his wings on the face of the earth.

I remembered then that our people who have crossed the big river to live in the West have said that no mountains exist there. I realized that

I would be lonely with no mountains to comfort me, and I hoped the white leaders would not force us to leave our homeland.

When the sun dipped behind the edge of the distant ridge, I determined that Raven should ride on the horse if we were to arrive before dark, so I removed the bundles from Red Sky's back, and Raven mounted the horse.

When we reached a steep place where a sycamore tree grew, Raven said, "The town is just beyond." And sure enough, when we crested the rise, a large tract of grassy, flat land greeted us. My breath drew in sharply, for spread out in front of us was an entire village.

For a brief moment, I felt as if I were approaching the village of my early childhood. A group of Cherokee children played in a field to the right. Twenty to thirty houses were scattered about, and they were not built with the edges fitted together but were constructed of long poles made from saplings. The walls were made of clapboard and the roofs of bark shingle. Beside each home was a smaller dwelling—the asi—the winter house. The asi is small and hugs the ground. I had not seen one for a long time. They were dug out, I remembered, and you could not stand in them. You could only sit or lie down, but always they were warm and were the favorite place of the old people in the cold winter months.

I could see also the council house with its circular shape in the middle of the village. A tall pole, with the white flag of peace flying at the top, stood near the entrance. The children on the field were playing chungke, throwing their spears at rolling, flat stones. I laughed at the younger children, for some of them were not wearing clothes, and the older boys wore only loincloths.

I sighed a long sigh and slowly turned a full circle. The lightness and joy I felt expanded with each breath and soon filled my whole being. I thought that if I spread my arms and patted the air softly, I would surely rise like a bird and circle easily over the entire village. I had not had such a feeling for a long time.

The boys, meanwhile, stopped their game and turned their gazes toward us. Two of them dropped their sticks and ran to us. They stared at Raven's wrapped arm and at the slashes on her face.

"Go to the home of Turtle Woman," Raven instructed them, "and tell my daughter that her mother is hurt and needs her assistance to get to the house."

The children ran toward the village.

Raven looked at me and asked, "Why are you smiling?"

"I like this town," I replied. "It is good that we are here."

"You should smile more often, Dancing Leaf."

SPIDER WOMAN

In the beginning, the world was cold; there was no fire. The Thunders, who live in Galunlati, shot a lightning bolt into the bottom of a hollow sycamore that grew on a great island. The animals could see the smoke rising, but they did not know how to get to it because of the water surrounding it. They held a council.

The flying animals seemed the natural choice, so Raven went first. He soared above the waters and landed on the sycamore tree, but while he sat there, deciding how to retrieve the fire, his feathers were scorched black, and he quickly flew back without the fire. Screech Owl went next, but a blast of hot air burned his eyes. He managed to fly home, but still to this day his eyes are red. Hooting Owl and Horned Owl tried next, but they came back with white rings around their eyes from the ashes carried up by the wind.

The elder animals decided to send a different species. So Black Racer Snake darted through the water, slithered through the grasses, and entered the stump through a small hole. He was nearly burned to death. He managed to escape, but his body was charred black.

None of the animals could be persuaded after these failures, until finally the tiny Water Spider said she would go. Now, she was not only a very brave little spider, she was also a very smart one. And before she left, she thought, *How will I bring back the fire?* The answer soon came to her, and she spun a thread from her body and wove it into a tusti bowl, which she fastened on her back. She swam across the water, waded through the grass, took one coal from the burning fire, put it in her tusti bowl, and then swam back. Ever since, the people have had fire.

So it was that when all seemed hopeless, and even the bravest of the brave could not complete this feat, tiny Water Spider brought from her own being the means to retrieve the fire. Across the dark and cold water, she cradled the container as a mother carries a child, and thus she wove her miracle; it was she who spun the web of life.

Chapter 5

We continued toward the heart of the village; Raven rode Red Sky and I led in front. The children scampered back to their game when Raven reminded them it was impolite to fix their eyes on elders.

Turtle, who was much smaller than Raven, came rushing from one of the huts with a man I judged to be her husband. "Mother! Mother! What has happened? Your arm is bandaged; your face is scratched."

Turtle's husband helped Raven off the horse, and Turtle put her arm around her mother's waist and patted her comfortingly. Red Hawk announced his name, asked mine, and took the reins of the horse. Raven began talking immediately about the ride and the frightening scene with the bear. She demanded that Red Hawk take several braves and retrieve the wagon at that very moment.

"No, Mother," he answered, "you can already see the Dog Star, and we will be unable to return before dark."

"But what if it rains and ruins my cloth? What if someone steals the iron kettles?"

"It will not rain, and no thieving Unakas live in this area."

As we walked, Raven continued in her moaning. I, from behind, watched how kind and gentle Turtle was with her mother and was relieved to think that I would not have to tolerate another difficult one like Raven. Red Hawk walked close beside me. He asked about my family and then asked how we had managed to get away from the bear. I told him about charging forward, throwing rocks, yelling my challenge, and finally seeing the baby bear. He handed me the reins and danced a war dance around me.

"Ah, Dancing Leaf, how brave you are! You did not even think about the bear attacking you? Mother," he called to Raven, "you have a strong, true friend."

But Raven stopped and turned a scowling face toward me. "It is for Dancing Leaf that I make this journey. Because of her bad dreams we have come to ask the services of the adawehi." She waited until Red Hawk and I had come abreast of them. "And what thanks do I receive?" Raven threw up the arm that had not been stricken. "Dancing Leaf did not listen when I protested stopping at the river. Because of her stubbornness I carry these deep wounds."

I gave the reins back to Red Hawk, and we walked in silence until Raven once again began muttering grievances to her daughter, but she talked low, and I could not hear what she said. I kept my eyes on my moccasined feet. Being with Raven was even more tiring than being with Jonathan, I judged. At least with Jonathan I could argue, but Raven was an elder to be respected.

When I stumbled, Red Hawk handed the reins to Turtle Woman and swooped me up. "Here, I will carry you. You must rest." He walked with large, quick strides so that we were ahead of the others, and he said in a comforting voice, "Raven's words can be like poison darts. In my early days with her, I only survived by pretending I had the impenetrable skin of the Uktena snake and that she could never find my seventh spot."

I laughed and knew again I would like Coosa Town.

We reached the hut, and Raven insisted that Red Hawk retrieve the adawehi immediately. Turtle had a looking glass, and Raven cried out when she saw her face. Turtle's two small ones were toddling about, unsteady on their feet. Frightened by their grandmother's cry, they began to whimper.

"Dancing Leaf," Raven ordered, "you will watch the twins while Turtle attends to me."

I was glad of this task because I loved small children, and I took them outside to walk about. They were beautiful with large, dark eyes and fat, round legs. They looked so much alike I could hardly tell them apart, but I knew from Raven's talk that one was a boy and the other a girl.

The adawehi, Talking River, arrived soon enough. I was surprised by his looks. He was a white hair, and he was tall and handsome, his back straight, his shoulders broad. Lame Deer, the adawehi who lived near us, was a small man with a back bent like a willow branch and a fluted voice, and I had imagined it was thus with all of the medicine men.

"A bear, Raven?" Talking River questioned. "Bear claws wound deeply. We must take care to prevent any red swelling or cloudy sap from the wounds. Let us see." He slowly unwound the cloths. "Ah, you have applied root paste already. That is good. How were you so wise to do this?"

"She did it," Raven said, gesturing to me without announcing my name.

"Ah, and who is this young maiden?"

Raven opened her mouth to reply, but my words spilled out quickly, "I am Dancing Leaf, daughter of Nanyehi, beloved woman of the wolf clan."

"Ah . . . yes." Talking River paused, his face full of interest. "I knew Nanyehi. She was a much respected beloved woman."

"Dancing Leaf was an orphan child," Raven interrupted, "adopted by our beloved woman."

"An adopted daughter? It is always good we can choose our children, and I am sure Nanyehi chose well. Do you know that Attakullakulla, the great peace chief, was an adopted member of our tribe? I am told he was born a Delaware. He was perhaps our finest leader in years past."

"Yes," I answered, glad to include my own knowledge. "Attakullakulla was uncle to Nanyehi, my mother, and father to Dragging Canoe, the great warrior. Mother told me many stories of Attakullakulla."

"What about my face?" Raven interrupted impatiently. "You must do something about these gashes on my face. I do not wish to be scarred."

Talking River took Raven's chin and tilted it upward while he examined the two streaks on her cheek. "They will mend easily enough. You may have scars, but they will be slight ones. You must not talk for a few days," he added, "so the skin will stay together."

I could not chase away the smile from my face, and when I looked about, I saw that Turtle and Red Hawk were turning their faces so Raven would not see their own smiles.

Talking River, however, maintained a serious countenance, and he instructed Turtle to bring boiling water from the iron kettle above the fire. He took flakes of red root from his medicine bag; I had seen such flakes before and thought they were bamboo briar. He worked quietly, mashing them with a small pestle, then mixing in drops of water. With light, thin strokes of the turkey feather, he painted Raven's arm and cheek. Then he pronounced sacred words four times as he faced each of the directions. Finally, he blew upon the wounded skin with his own breath. The deeper scratches on the arm he wrapped again.

"For three days you must keep your arm still," he warned. "You don't want to anger the cuts or cause the blood to flow."

"Three days!" Raven exclaimed. "I have much sewing to do while I am here. I must do my sewing."

"Again," he reminded her in a voice of soft thunder, "you must not talk." He looked at her for a moment and then at our faces, which still tried not to smile. "I will leave tea leaves for Turtle Woman to brew," he told Raven. "You will drink this tea three times a day, and this will cause you to sleep for long hours. You must do this so you will have a restful time."

Talking River took her outside, where he sang a song to the earth, to the river, to the stones, and to the woods. He addressed the immortal creatures who lived in the sky—the yellow wolf, the yellow otter, and the yellow buzzard—and asked them to come down and heal Raven's wounds. When he finished, he instructed her to go inside and rest.

She opened her mouth to reply, but when the adawehi's eyes grew wide, she shut it. She tried to speak without moving her lips, and her words sounded like someone was holding a cloth over her mouth. "Take Dancing Leaf with you," she muttered.

I knew what she was saying, but Talking River stared at her sternly.

"Tell him!" she commanded me, her words muffled by her closed lips.

"I come for bad dreams," I explained, my own voice low.

54

"Ah, then you will come with me," the adawehi said as he gathered up his things. "You will stay with me and my wife, Spider Woman."

As we walked to his hut, he asked questions about my dreams. I explained about the monsters that appeared and caused me to yell out and wake up Long Fellow. "I would not come just for myself," I added. "The old one needs his sleep."

"Ah, yes, I see."

Spider Woman, like her husband, was an elder. Her nearly snow-white hair had only scattered threads of black. She wore it plaited down her back. She was round in shape, and her gestures and smiles were large. "It will be good to have a young maiden staying with us."

Her words surprised me, and perhaps she read my thoughts, because she quickly added, "You will stay here with us for as long as it takes. Raven is recovering from her wounds, and my husband tells me she has taken on the manners of a wounded bear herself. We will leave her to the care of her daughter."

For the third time since my arrival, a feeling of peace settled over me and I knew I would love this place.

Talking River was not a man to waste time, and he began the remedy at once, brewing a tea made with spine leaf. Only a short time after drinking the steaming liquid, I had to rise and run behind the hut, and there it all came back up. I was ashamed, but Spider Woman was behind me and said, "The medicine is working. Whatever is causing bad dreams will now pass from you."

Two more times I ran outside. After that I slept a long, deep sleep, but I had gnawing pains throughout the night. When I awoke in the morning, Spider Woman said I had cried out several times.

I wished I could remember what I had dreamed, because both Spider Woman and Talking River asked many questions as if it were important. How strange, I thought, that I could not remember these dreams now, when I could not make myself forget the dreams I experienced at home.

"I am sorry to have awakened you," I apologized. "Perhaps I should sleep outside."

"It is our work," Talking River assured me. "We will stay near you, observe your reactions, and that is how we will determine the correct remedy."

My eyes filled with misty dampness. I remembered the days long ago when I had first come to live with Beloved Mother as a small child. For many nights she had tended me, wrapping me in her long arms and rocking gently until the demons of my sleep world had departed. And now these two were giving up their nights of sleep to help me. They were like grandparents, caring for a troubled granddaughter.

Talking River excused himself to call on Raven and his other patients, and Spider Woman and I washed the bowls from our breakfast of corn mush.

"Do you always work together?" I asked Spider Woman while we rubbed the bowls clean. "I know only one adawehi, Lame Deer, and I have only seen him work alone."

"My husband worked alone when we had children at home. But I quietly listened and observed. In the last few years, I have often helped, so now it feels natural to work with him. Sometimes I even hear voices from the spirit world, telling me what needs to be done. I do not say the medicine words, though, as he is the only one who has been properly taught."

Spider Woman and I spent the day sewing, for she insisted that I be a full Cherokee here and leave the Unaka world behind. We made a dress of deerskin, using fishbone needles and sinew thread. All the while we worked, she asked questions. "Do you have a cat? That could be the cause of your trouble. Cherokees should never have cats. Do you have pigs? You must never eat of the pig, or it will make you fat and lazy like the pig. Do you observe the proper petitions to the animal spirits when killing for food? What about the fire in your hearth—has it come from the sacred fire of seven woods rekindled in the Green Corn Festival?"

I was glad that we had no cat and glad also that we no longer had pigs. Always, she cautioned, we Cherokee must observe the teachings of our ancestors and turn our backs on Unaka ways. Only then would our lives be free and healthy again.

She thought my dreams might originate with some bird or animal that had been offended by my relatives. "When you were small, did your mother tell you the screech owl would get you if you cried at night?" she asked. "If so, that may have angered members of the bird clan and they would then be causing these gnawing pains."

I told her I did not know, that I did not remember the days when I was a small child and lived in a small village much like Coosa Town.

Talking River, like his wife, thought my dreams might be coming from angered animal creatures taking their vengeance, so for the next two evenings we observed the proper ritual for driving out these spirits. I sat up, facing the direction of the setting sun, while Talking River recited the words of the sacred formula: "Listen! Ha! I am a great adawehi! I never fail in anything. It is a mere hooting owl that has frightened this one. Ha! I have now put it in the spruce thicket. There it is bound and there it shall remain."

He then blew upon my neck with a rod made of trumpetweed. "Listen! Ha! I am a great adawehi! I never fail in anything. I surpass all others. It is only a screech owl that has frightened her. Ha! Now I have put it in the laurel thicket. There it must remain."

He blew upon my left shoulder. "Listen! Ha! I am a great adawehi! I never fail in anything. I surpass all others. It is only a small rabbit that has scared this one. I put it behind the mountain ridge. It may never cross again. It is gone from my sight."

Then he blew upon my right shoulder. "Listen! Ha! I am a great adawehi! I never fail in anything. I surpass all others. It is only a mountain sprite that has scared this one. Undoubtedly this is what has frightened her. I put it high on the bluff. There he must remain because I have caused it to be so."

Finally he blew across my chest.

I was glad that it was a simple ritual. Sometimes the healing ceremonies involved scratching with bear claws and trips to the cold mountain springs, but I remained in the hut as he performed the rite.

Talking River made visits to Raven each day to attend to her healing. He fasted for one full day and recited special formulas to the bear clan, whom we must have angered. The bear must be assured of our good intentions, he counseled, or we would risk another attack.

Spider Woman and I turned our attention to many tasks. "Always, you should be busy," she said, "making things with your hands. This brings peace to the mind. How do you spend your time at home?"

"I do many things," I answered. "I tend the garden, gather herbs and berries, and prepare food." I did not tell her I milked the cow or fed the chickens and gathered eggs. These were things from the Unaka world, and I knew she would not approve.

"Do you pound your corn, or do you send it to the mill?" she asked.

"I pound the corn," I answered truthfully, although in years past, Beloved Mother and I had sometimes taken the corn to the Unaka mill.

"That is good. Selu, the corn maiden, has heard that some of her people are taking their corn to the mill. She cries in pain, saying her children are grinding her very bones when they do this. Our people must stop this practice and return to the old ways.

"Do you listen to stories?" she asked.

"Yes," I again answered truthfully. "I love stories. When I was small, always I begged my elders to tell me stories, and they sometimes became annoyed. I know many Cherokee stories." I did not tell her I was recording the stories on paper, and I was glad I had not brought my writing paper with me.

Quickly Spider Woman went through a list of stories—how the world was made, how the Cherokee obtained corn and fire, what the stars are like, the Pleiades and the pine, the Milky Way, and the great flood. Yes, I assured her, I knew all of these and another ten or so that she mentioned. She listened attentively as I repeated several of them for her and was pleased that I knew them well.

Over the next few days, she shared many stories with me that I had never heard before—the rattlesnake's revenge, the katydid's warning, the bride from the South, the haunted whirlpool, and others—and so I listened carefully and could hardly believe my good fortune to find someone who loved the stories as much as I did. As we worked, she recited and I repeated back. At night before I went to sleep, I said the stories in my mind again so I would not forget them.

Of course, all this time we were telling stories, we were busy with our hands. When the days for performing the healing rituals were passed, we attended to the matter of making baskets, a task I had watched often but had never done myself. We gathered river cane from the nearby stream and spent the morning trimming and scraping. We hung the splints in the sun to dry. On the next day we began the process of dying for color. We used three large pots; in one we boiled black walnut root, and in the next yellow root, and in the third blood-root for red. For half a day we stirred the splints in the simmering pots until they emerged in strong hues of black, yellow, and dark red. Children from the village gathered while we worked.

"We come every day when our mothers allow it," Laughing Girl informed me.

We gave the children corn cakes dabbed with honey, and then I let them take turns stirring the pot. Laughing Girl argued with her cousin, Morning Dove, over whose turn was longer. When Morning Dove pushed Laughing Girl to the ground, I scolded them both and told them they must go home, but Spider Woman came forward and took each child by the hand.

"We will attend to this in a different manner," she said to me. "Now, Laughing Girl and Morning Dove, you must go lie down in the shade of the hut on the other side. There you will set your eyes upon the sky and search for clouds. You must lie very still and pay attention to these clouds. If you are quiet and respectful, then the clouds will make pictures and tell you stories. You may return when you have a story to share with us."

As they scurried off like squirrels, anxious to begin their task, Spider Woman turned to me and said, "Cherokee children are to be treated always with gentleness, even when correcting them. Have you been to the Unaka school?" she asked suspiciously.

"Yes, I have been there," I answered, not saying that I had lived at the mission school for three winters. I hoped she would not ask me more.

"Well, you must not do as the Unakas do. I have seen how harshly they treat their own children. I am told that young ones in the mission schools are sometimes whipped. This should never be. Young hearts are connected closely to the spirit world from which they came, and we must take care to honor the spirit in each child."

I had heard of these whippings, too, although I had never been whipped, nor did Father Gambold or Mother Gambold whip any of the children when I was at Spring Place. But I was told by older children that in the early days, small children were whipped and the practice wasn't stopped until several Cherokee chiefs held council with the teachers and demanded that the children not be treated in such a harsh manner.

The two girls returned after a short while, giggling and holding hands. Laughing Girl had seen a small rabbit lazily nibbling on a blade of grass in her cloud pictures. Morning Dove had watched a canoe filled with singing children float across the sky. The other children then all insisted they must lie down to study the clouds, and the entire afternoon was filled with cloud stories as we dyed the strips of cane.

The next two days were spent weaving our baskets. We gave the children smaller pieces of cane and taught them how to make mats. Talking River stopped to visit in the afternoon, and he wove the splints together to make dolls for the younger girls.

We began by weaving winnowing baskets—long baskets with flat bottoms and small sides—used for sifting grain. I had only one winnowing basket and decided to make this one a tighter weave for making finer flour. I wove bands of red and black into my basket and thought I had created a fine basket and wished that Beloved Mother could see it.

Finally we made doubleweave baskets. A doubleweave basket, Spider Woman informed me, is a basket within a basket. I followed her movements as I wove my own. We began at the bottom and wove up all four sides to the rim, where we bent the splints outward and then wove down the sides, creating our double basket.

"No doubt," Spider Woman remarked, "this is the tusti bowl Water Spider created when she returned with fire. This basket can withstand both water and fire."

I was so proud of my basket, I could hardly put it down. I carried it with me for half a day, showing it to other women of the village, who praised my work.

"You must come back in the cool months, and I will teach you how to make clay pots," Spider Woman insisted. "It is too hot to make pots at this time."

"Yes," I agreed, glad to have a reason for returning and pleased that I should be asked to.

Six days and nights had passed since we arrived in Coosa Town, and I had slept peacefully for the past several evenings. On the seventh day, Talking River assured me that Raven's wounds were healing and that she was ready to travel back to our village. He, meanwhile, had been called to a neighboring village to attend to a sick child with mountain fever.

I bid him farewell and promised that I would visit in the cool months of autumn. I gave him a small deerskin pouch that I had made when I made my dress. It was small and could only hold medicine roots. I was embarrassed that I had such a small offering, for many times adawehis received large bundles of deerskin or rabbit fur. But he seemed pleased and immediately filled it with yellow root and snake remedy. He attached a thong of deer hide so he could wear it with the other pouches around his neck.

Spider Woman and I made a large fire outside the hut that night, and we stayed up for many hours repeating stories. We sprinkled tobacco on the fire before retiring and offered prayers for my safe passage back to Long Fellow's cabin. The moon that night was once again a full, round moon, and I thought of the last full moon when Blue Lake left for Virginia. Surely he was there now at this very moment. I hoped that he was standing on the porch of his father's house, gazing at this moon and thinking of me as I was thinking of him now. I sprinkled another pinch of tobacco into the fire and said a silent prayer for his safekeeping.

When we had retired to our sleeping mats, Spider Woman spoke softly to me, "Dancing Leaf, you can remain here and live with us if you want. I have sensed that you are not happy with your life. Talking River and I have both discussed this, and you are welcome."

"How kind of you!" I replied, drawing up to a sitting position. "I would love to stay here for many days and nights . . . but I have my uncle to think about, and the others, too."

"I did not think you would say yes," Spider Woman confided. "And yet I thought you needed to know that we would be happy to have you share our home. In future days perhaps you may wish to return."

I did not know what to say then, so I rose from my sleeping mat and went over and put my arms around her, and we hugged each other as tears once again spilled onto my cheeks.

But that night, I did not sleep well. At one time, I sat up straight and turned my head from side to side, listening for the crying voice I had heard.

Spider Woman was awake then, too. "What is it?"

"Did you hear?" I asked. "A child is crying out to me. She needs help, but no one is there to help her. She is alone."

"No one is crying out, Dancing Leaf. The child is in your dream." But Spider Woman did not say, "Go back to sleep." Instead she rose and came over to me and asked, "Do you know the child?"

I shook my head and struggled to remember clearer details of the dream.

"Sit quietly," she said, "and try to remember as much as you can. We must find this lost child. I'll return with a helper."

She rose and went into the room where Talking River kept herbs and medicines. She returned with a wrapped bundle. Carefully she unwrapped the cloth, and I gasped when I saw the crystal lying there. It was the size of a large potato, and it was clear quartz. She handed it to me, and I held it as one might hold a newborn infant.

"Hold it close to your heart for a few moments," she instructed.

I brought my hand to my chest.

"Now, look into the crystal and see if you can find the crying child."

When I looked, I saw a girl, a very small girl. She was sitting amongst the high reeds growing along a creek. Her knees were drawn up, and she was sitting very still. Her lips did not move, and no sound came from her mouth, but words came from her mind, and I could hear them: *Mother, where are you? Please help me! Please find me. I am afraid.* All of this I recited to Spider Woman.

"Who is this child?" she asked.

"I am that child," I said, surprised at my answer. "I cannot cry out loud because I have been instructed not to or the Unakas will find me and kill me."

"Why is the child not with her mother?"

"Her mother has gone to look for her little brother. The little girl . . . I mean . . . *I* have been sitting there for a long while, and still her mother has not returned."

"You must go to this child and comfort her," Spider Woman said gently. "Tell her that Mother is gone and Little Brother also. They are now in Galunlati with other departed Cherokee. Someday the child will see her again. But now the mother and brother are looking down at her, and they want her to know they are happy. They are in a place of peace. They are saving a place for her."

I sent the child these thoughts, and she quieted for a moment, but then she looked up at me and again I could hear her thoughts.

"She is afraid," I told Spider Woman. "She does not want to be without a mother. Who will take care of her? Who will be her family? She is too small to take care of herself."

"You will take care of her," Spider Woman assured me. "You must tell her that."

I looked at Spider Woman. "But I am that child," I protested softly.

"Yes. Tell her that you have become a strong person and you can take care of her. Tell her you found another mother and another family. Tell her you have learned to do many things. You can scare bears. You can cook food and make baskets and clothing. Many other things you can do. She must be at peace because she will be cared for."

I recited these things to the child much as Spider Woman had said them. The child lay down and soon enough was in a peaceful sleep. And so were Spider Woman and I. When I awoke early the next morning, Spider Woman was lying beside me, but the large crystal was not there.

"I have a crystal of my own," I told Spider Woman as we sipped blackberry tea. I removed the blue cloth from the pouch around my waist, unwrapped the crystal, and showed it to her.

"A beautiful crystal," she said, turning it in her hand. "Was it your mother's?"

"No, a friend gave it to me."

"Always a crystal is given for a special purpose, even though we may not know it." Spider Woman held it skyward. "A crystal has a special spirit of its own, and it is connected to the star spirits from whence our people came." A frown formed on her face. "The crystal is a tired crystal now. Have you cleansed it?"

"No. I did not know to do so."

"First, this crystal must rest in the sun." She opened the door and positioned the crystal so that the healing rays of the sun could reach it. "You must find a sturdy cedar branch," she instructed.

When I returned with one, we placed it in the fire. Spider Woman passed the crystal through the smoke in a small circle from east to west then from west to east, and I repeated this action several times.

"Now we go to the stream," she declared.

We walked in bare feet so the fresh dew would not wet our moccasins. The mists of morning were still clinging to the flowing waters. We placed the crystal in a shallow place, and then we sat near the edge to wait.

"The river of life will cleanse the crystal," Spider Woman promised. "Any bad thoughts and actions surrounding the crystal will now be washed away."

When we removed the crystal, we set it upon a rock to let it dry. Spider Woman took a kernel of corn from her medicine pouch and handed it to me.

"Place the kernel on the crystal and offer a prayer of thanks."

Carefully I balanced the corn on top of the crystal. "Thank you, crystal being, for coming to me. I will take care of you well. I will be your friend."

Spider Woman nodded approvingly. "Now you must wrap it back in the blue cloth and keep it covered in a safe place. The crystal must rest there for two full days. Then you may remove it and wear it close to your body in a waist pouch or close to your heart in a medicine pouch."

So I wrapped the crystal and placed it deep inside my satchel. Spider Woman and I then walked slowly to the home of Turtle. I was wearing my deerskin dress and hoped that Raven would not be so rude as to make a laughing comment about it. We walked silently, having no more need for words. It was a sacred time, this walk with Spider Woman. Our thoughts and our hearts were together in peace. Our bodies moved easily, freely, as in a gentle dance. With each step, I felt the pulsing of the earth. Even our breathing was in rhythm, echoing the mountain breeze that lightly cooled our faces.

Before we reached Turtle's home, though, Spider Woman turned and faced me. "I will go no farther," she said. "You go ahead to the others to make your preparations for travel."

"Thank you, Mother," I said, for in the old villages it is proper to call all women helpers *Mother*. "I will not forget your kindness. Thank you for the stories. Thank you for the healing."

We embraced gently for a moment, and then I remembered that I had no gift for Spider Woman. "I will return with a gift in the time of falling leaves," I promised.

"You must come, but you will not bring a gift," she insisted. "We are all asked to be helpers in this world. Your gift to me is to give something to someone else. When you have done this, you will have found your own true path as a helper."

I thanked her again, and then she turned and walked back toward her hut. I watched as four children quickly gathered around her.

"Can we make baskets today?" asked Blue Leaf.

"Today we will gather corn and then we will pound it," she replied, placing her arms around two of the children. The other two skipped ahead and picked flowers for her.

I hoped that I would someday be as she was, with children happily bounding alongside.

"Ah, Dancing Leaf," Raven called to me as I approached. "I was wise to insist upon bringing the wagon. Turtle and her babies will return with us. We have so many bundles to take. And also I bring a bundle for the bear," she said, smiling.

Turtle and Red Hawk were heaping the bundles upon the wagon.

"How long will Turtle stay with us?" I asked, startled by the news.

"Who knows?" Raven answered easily. "Red Hawk will be gone for many months. He travels with a delegation of Cherokee to Washington to speak with the white father."

I had not seen Raven smiling for some time, and I was glad that she was in good spirits, but my heart was racing. What work it would be to get Raven, Turtle, the children, and all their belongings back to the farm! But then I saw how quickly Turtle darted about with bundles on her back and babies in her arms, always mindful of what was around, and I thought *Turtle Woman* was the wrong name for her; perhaps she, too, should have been called *Spider Woman*.

I looked carefully at Raven's arm. It showed no evidence of redness or swelling, but I could plainly see a thick line of new skin where the flesh had pulled together. The scars on her cheek were no wider than a thread, although she made sad noises in her throat when she showed them to me.

Before long we had all of the bundles loaded in the wagon. Turtle sat among them, her babies on her lap, and Raven and I rode on the bench.

Red Hawk went with us as far as the spreading sycamore, then he bid us a safe journey and waved good-bye to his wife and children. "I will see you by the time of the first snow," he promised.

By the first snow? Would it be that long? But snow fell earlier in the mountains, I reminded myself.

We traveled happily enough. The air was cool, and Turtle sang songs to the little ones. When we spotted a terrapin crossing the road, we picked him up to be a companion for the children. Soon all was quiet again, and we rode in silence as the babies napped. I went over the stories in my mind—stories about how the rabbit tricked the bear, how the deer got his horns, why the mole lives under the ground, how the unhappy wife returned with strawberries for her husband.

We stopped to rest and refresh ourselves. It was not in the same place we had stopped before, but I learned then what Raven had brought for the bear, for she produced a foul smelling bag and tied it to a tree.

"What is in the bag?" I asked.

"A mixture of herbs, bark, and root," she answered. "It will keep the bears away."

Turtle had packed strips of dried rabbit meat for our lunch, and Spider Woman had sent corn cakes drizzled with honey. We took some time to rest and stretch out, and then I began thinking about the past week with the villagers of Coosa Town.

I had lived there for seven days, eating their food and wearing their clothes. Like the boy in the bear story, I realized I had found a good place to live. In many ways life there was simpler than my life at our cabin beside the Ocoee River, but I knew that if I stayed in Coosa Town much longer, I would be like the boy who lived with the bears and soon enough became one of them.

As much as I loved living in that world with grandmothers and grandfathers and children all around, I could not return to stay. Suddenly I realized that I was still wearing the deerskin dress, and I went to the wagon and took out my brown skirt and my white blouse. I put them on, even though the brown skirt had ragged edges where I had torn strips to bind Raven's arm.

Spider Woman's words came to me: *We must turn our back on the Unaka customs and insist that our people follow the old ways.* But many of the Unaka customs had now become part of my life. Beloved Mother herself had insisted that we must learn from the Unakas and adopt the good things they offered to us.

"We are the wolf clan," she often reminded me. "The wolf is a creature of survival because he can adapt to the cold snow of the mountain or the steamy heat of the swamps. Like the wolf, we must adapt to our surroundings if we are to survive as a people."

We rested until the sun traveled past the midpoint of day. I was glad we had brought the foul smelling bag but also glad to leave it behind. We saw no bears that day and proceeded on our journey.

The sun was resting on the tops of the trees when we crossed the meadow and Long Fellow's cabin came into view. We reached the grove of pine trees, but Chera did not come out to meet us. I wondered where she was.

How the World Was Made

At one time all the creatures lived above in the great sky vault—Galunlati. But things became crowded, and they worried that soon there would not be enough room for everyone. They peered down, and all below was water, not a place they could live. They wondered what was below the surface, so Little Water Beetle volunteered to go down. She came back with a piece of mud, which began to grow and spread until it became an island of land.

Several members of the bird clan flew down next, but the earth was too soft and wet to land, so they returned. Great Buzzard volunteered to go down and survey the situation. He became so tired when he reached the Cherokee country that his great wings flapped and struck the ground, creating valleys and ridges. That is why the Cherokee country is a land of mountains.

Finally the earth dried, but the sky was dark. The animals set the sun in motion to travel east to west, so that the earth beings would have light. The animals and plants were the first to come down to earth, and then man.

Now this new homeland was firmly attached with strongly woven cords to each corner of the sky vault. If the world grows old and worn out, or if it becomes too crowded and heavy, then the cords will break, and the earth will sink down into the ocean. The people are afraid of this.

The Great One informed the creatures that these cords would only hold the world as long as everything remained in sacred balance. All beings—four-legged, two-legged, many-legged, no-legged, and the winged ones—must live in harmony, dependent upon each other for life and new birth.

Chapter 6

When we reached the small grove of pines, we could see Five Killer and Long Fellow sitting in their rocking chairs on the porch. Five Killer was quick to motion, running out to meet us and whooping as he advanced. Long Fellow could not be in such a hurry, but he, too, stepped off the porch and, in his slow shuffle run, made it half the distance to the wagon. When Five Killer was alongside, I pulled the reins and Red Sky stopped.

Five Killer reached for Raven and twirled her in a full circle before setting her down. "Why have you been so long?" he demanded. "If you had not returned today, I would be leaving myself to retrieve you."

Raven said nothing, but with eyebrows rising like mountain peaks, she held up her bandaged arm for Five Killer's inspection.

"What has happened?" he cried. "Raven, you have been injured?"

"I was attacked!" she said dramatically, as she unwound the cloth so that he could see the healing streaks.

"Those are deep wounds." He held her arm, gently stroking his finger along the thick, pink scars. "Was it a panther?"

"A bear," she said quietly. "And my face, too, has been marred with scratches." Pulling back the scarf that she had draped around her head, she turned her face so her scars were clearly visible. For a moment my heart sank with the weight of her own, because I knew how deeply troubled she was by these imperfections to her beauty.

Five Killer cradled her face in his hands and squinted as he looked at her cheek. "Scratches?" he asked. "What scratches? I see only two lines, finer than a hair's width, and they will soon be gone."

He placed small kisses about her face then and murmured words we did not hear. Turtle and I turned away and began to busy ourselves. We lifted the children from the wagon to the ground, but they wrapped themselves in our skirts and peered shyly out at these new people and new surroundings.

"How good to see you, Five Killer," Turtle said at the first quiet moment.

"Ah, Turtle," Five Killer said. "I must apologize for not offering my greetings. How kind of you to travel with your mother to see that she has made a safe trip."

Raven quickly spoke. "Turtle will be staying with us for a while."

At this news, Five Killer looked to me, and I could see a cloud of unease in his eyes.

I took Red Sky by the reins and began walking toward Long Fellow, who waited beneath the sycamore. Again my eyes searched the landscape, but Chera was not in sight, and I wondered why she had not come to greet us.

"Uncle, you must meet Raven's kind daughter," I said after I embraced Long Fellow. "This is Turtle Woman, and these are her twins, Running Deer and Little Fawn."

Long Fellow smiled as he always did when he saw small children. His smile began at the face and spread throughout his body. "You may call me Grandfather," he said to Turtle.

He stooped forward and picked up Little Fawn. The action surprised me, for Long Fellow's frame is frail and bent, but he did so easily enough. Little Fawn made no protest and reached out her hand and touched his cheek.

As we proceeded toward the cabin, Raven recounted the story of the bear attack. The bear, she claimed, was at least seven feet tall and her roar could be heard echoing across the mountain ridges. Her legs were as large as tree stumps, and her claws could rip off the face of a mountain lion. Raven changed the facts so that she was the one who yelled at the bear while I was meandering down the stream with no knowledge of the danger. At least she did not claim to be the one who threw rocks, but then she gave me no credit for that either.

Five Killer praised her brave actions, then he turned to Turtle. "Thank you, Turtle, for bringing your mother home to me. How long can you stay with us?"

"My husband travels to Washington with a delegation of Cherokee men. We may not see him again until the time of snow."

"He would not leave you for that long!" Five Killer protested.

"The journey is a long one, Five Killer," Raven said, her voice light as a feather floating to the ground. "My daughter is a fine cook," she added. "She makes corn bread and venison stew and honey cakes and sweet potato pie and many other good things."

"Is that so?" he asked.

"Yes, and we have Dancing Leaf to help with the babies."

I did not mind helping, but I did mind that Raven decided so.

We rounded the bend, and Long Fellow's cabin came into view again, but when my eyes shifted to the hill behind it, Five Killer's cabin was no longer there. I saw only a darkened mound.

"What has happened to your cabin?" I asked, my voice sounding like a bleating deer. Yet even as I asked the question, I knew the answer, for a sharp scent traveled with the winds. "Your cabin has burned down!" I exclaimed.

"Burned down? Five Killer, what has happened?" Raven cried. She stretched her eyes to search the distance, and I could see the terror in them. "Is everything lost? What about my spinning wheel and loom?"

Five Killer raised his arms to the sky. "Raven, I do not know how it happened. Perhaps a burning ember from the fire. It happened the very day you left, and we spotted it soon enough. The Unaka boy was here, and we pulled out your spinning wheel and loom. They are at Long Fellow's. Do not be so much distressed."

The little ones began whimpering at the disturbance of their elders, and I helped Turtle lift them back into the wagon. She climbed in with them and comforted them with corn cakes, and slowly we all began to move forward again.

"But where will we stay?" demanded Raven, uttering the question that was in all of our minds. "Already I was worried that with Turtle and the children we would be crowded, but now what will we do? We cannot all stay in Long Fellow's cabin."

"Only for a few days," Five Killer answered hurriedly. "We are working on the inn, and we are making fine rooms. Soon we will be able to make our home there. You will see."

Raven stomped her foot. "But we cannot live there. The inn is filled with rotting boards, and it smells like a river. Who knows what creatures have taken refuge there?" She looked suspiciously at Five Killer. "Besides, you do not know how to build an inn."

"Tomorrow you will see. We have been busily working since your departure. We have already patched the roof and put up more framework. Others from the village come daily to help."

I could not help but wonder who the others were, but still I was anxious for Chera. "Where is Chera?" I asked Long Fellow.

"Come, you will see." Long Fellow motioned, and we turned our footsteps toward the barn, while the others continued to the cabin.

I heard Chera's yelps of delight as we drew near, and when I turned the block of wood and released the door, she bounded out happily to see me. I bent down and let her lick my face while I observed the swelling under her belly—only it was not the swelling of the unborn, but instead the swelling that produces milk for young.

When Long Fellow pointed, my eyes followed his finger, and I saw two very small creatures in the open stall where the cow Susie once was kept. Susie had died last spring, and now we had only the brown and white cow, Rosie. Rosie turned her head around when I looked in her direction.

"You have been away too long," Long Fellow said. "Chera could not wait; she had them the day after you left for Coosa Town."

"They are so small," I said softly, as I made my way to where the puppies nested in straw. Their cries were like the mewing sounds of a cat. They did not stand up, but scooted around to find their mother. I picked one up and held it close to my body, and he quieted. With his eyes so tightly closed, I thought he resembled a small mouse. "How long before they can open their eyes?"

"Soon. In only a few weeks they will be jumping and tumbling about."

"Sifters or bows?" I asked, using the Cherokee expressions for *girls* and *boys*.

"That one is a sifter," he said, pointing to the one I held. She had a reddish coat, and I could see it was tipped with black like Chera's. "The other," he said, pointing to the speckled one, "is a bow."

"Only two?" I asked. "Such a small litter."

"A smaller, black one did not survive. He wasn't breathing when he was born. We could not revive him."

Chera nuzzled her head under my hand, and I petted her. "What fine puppies, Chera! How well you have done. Blue Lake will be pleased." As the last words tumbled from my lips, I felt the pain that crossed my heart when I thought of Blue Lake. Virginia—the word came to my mind, but I could only picture the lines drawn on the map. I turned my face so that Long Fellow would not see my troubling thoughts. "Has there been a letter?" My voice sounded like that of a child of five instead of a woman of sixteen years.

"A letter came, but it is not from Blue Lake," Long Fellow answered. "But you must write him and tell him about these new puppies."

"Yes, I can do that," I agreed.

"He will send a letter soon enough," Long Fellow assured, as though he could hear the thoughts in my head.

Rosie turned her head to me and mooed softly, and I went to her and checked her udders. "Well, someone has been milking you," I observed, pleased that she had no hard lumps. "So Five Killer has learned to milk a cow?" I asked Long Fellow.

"The Unaka boy comes every day to milk her," he answered.

"Jonathan?" My voice rose, and every pair of eyes in the barn turned toward me. Even the speckled hen strutted over, clucking as she walked. She cocked her head and fixed a large brown eye on me.

"Yes, he comes every morning when he's finished his work at home. He milks the cow and helps Five Killer to restore the inn."

"And why would he do that?"

"Perhaps we will let him use the inn on Sundays for the meeting house."

It is impolite to stare at elders, but I could not help myself. I wrapped my arms tightly around my chest and continued to stare until Long Fellow coughed, looked away, and mumbled, "He is a hard worker, that one. Five Killer would not let a Unaka take advantage."

A picture formed in my mind: Jonathan lifting heavy rocks, splitting wood, rolling logs, nailing boards. His face and body were wet with sweat. Five Killer stood idly by, drawing on his pipe as he pointed to the places that needed mending. He, of course, was not sweating.

A smile spread across my face, although I was still irritated that this thunder being could so easily accomplish his purpose. Besides, I did not wish to have to deal with him every day of the week. He would, no doubt, bring his black book and insist on reading passages to me. When he left his comb unattended, I decided, I would steal it. Perhaps I would throw it into the river.

I returned to Chera's puppies, kissed both of them, and murmured words of comfort. Chera's nose pushed against my hand, and I petted and praised her once again. Long Fellow turned the block of wood that held the door shut as we left.

When we reached the cabin, Turtle ladled squirrel stew into our bowls. Squash and potatoes simmered with the meat. The twins were seated on the floor with a small bowl in front of each of them. Five Killer sat with a spoon, feeding them alternately. They ate like greedy baby birds, having barely swallowed before their mouths were open again. Five Killer was amused, and he teased them gently as he fed them. Raven rested a hand on Five Killer's shoulder, and I noticed the contented smile on her face.

Although I did not like Raven, I could see the happiness when these two were together. Five Killer became more lively, his laziness bursting into activity, and Raven was like a peaceful, flowing river in his presence, and not the crashing waterfall she was at other times.

The next few days would not be so bad, I decided. Turtle and the twins could sleep in my room, and Raven, of course, would sleep with Five Killer in Long Fellow's room. Long Fellow could join me on the porch, where we would enjoy the view of moon and stars.

My peaceful thoughts were soon enough interrupted with Raven's words. "Dancing Leaf, the cabin will be crowded the next few days.

Jonathan travels back and forth every day. You would do well to go with him and stay with his family in the evenings."

My mouth opened, but no words came out; I did not know what to say. I looked to Five Killer; he no longer had a smile on his face and would not look at me.

Long Fellow broke the silence. His words were soft as always, but this time they were the softness of a distant thunder. "Raven, it would not be proper for Dancing Leaf to travel to the Unaka boy's to sleep. There is no need for her to leave her home. I will hear no more talk like this."

I let my breath out slowly, and a warm glow filled my heart. Long Fellow seldom spoke more than two sentences, but when he did, everyone listened. My eyes darted to Raven, but her head was bowed and I could not judge her expression.

"I will sleep on the porch," I offered simply and returned to my evening meal.

When I finished, I fetched Chera from the barn and together we went to my favorite place, the large, flattened rock on the side of the stream. I climbed up on it, clasped my knees, and gazed upward to the round, yellow moon. Would Blue Lake be here when the moon fully revealed her face again? Surely not. It would take longer than that to attend to his father's business, and besides, he could very well decide to stay in Virginia and live with his white family.

And maybe Raven was right. I must consider my own path in life. Although Long Fellow's words were kind, things were too crowded now, and perhaps I should be the one to leave. I did not like to have these confusing thoughts, and that is why I was sitting on the rock. Long Fellow had taught me the wisdom of "Grandfather Rock."

"If you sit very quietly," he counseled me in days past, "and raise your questions respectfully, Grandfather Rock will supply the answer."

In the past few years, I had often sat on Grandfather Rock with a question, and I was always rewarded with a reply. Of course, sometimes I did not hear the answer right away. Sometimes days passed before a solution came to me. I took a deep breath on this day, and my words poured forth: "What shall I do with my life, Grandfather Rock? Raven wants me to move. She complains our world is too crowded, when she is the one who has crowded our home. What is to be done?"

I stilled my body, sat up straight, and listened, but I heard no answer. I was bolder with my next question. "Grandfather Rock, if I were a brave, I would go on a vision quest. Why do not women go on these quests? We need answers, too."

I remained motionless and listened for a longer time, and this time I listened with my whole body. What I heard was the soft running of the waters beside me. I closed my eyes and listened more intently, and the trickle of the small stream became the rushing waters of a swollen mountain stream. I could hear other noises, too, and they became louder and clearer, and I knew that I had heard them before. And then suddenly I recognized them—they were the sounds I had heard the last day in my village when the Unaka soldiers attacked. They were the sounds of rifles firing and flames crackling and people crying.

When I was first rescued, I often heard these sounds at night, and I could only go to sleep by holding my hands over my ears. Often I cried out and screamed. The other children in the orphan lodge could not tolerate such alarming sounds at sleeping time, so Beloved Mother took me into her cabin, where she rocked and comforted me until I fell back into a restful sleep.

But on this day as I sat on Grandfather Rock, I did not put my hands to my ears. Instead I reached for the crystal and pressed it against my heart and listened. I listened because I hoped to hear the voice of my mother and also my brother. I listened bravely until the noises had all died down, but still I heard no voices. Perhaps, I reasoned, I did not hear my mother or my brother because they had escaped to the nearby mountains. Was that the message of Grandfather Rock?

I opened my eyes when I felt the gentle pressure of a hand upon my head. I looked into the face of Five Killer, and I remembered looking into the same face many years before when he lifted my body from the reeds and placed me on his horse. But the Five Killer I saw today had hair the color of ashes and eyes surrounded by folds of skin; he was not the younger man of years past.

"What are you dreaming about?" he asked as he swung his legs around the rock and cradled his body behind mine.

"Many things," I answered.

"So, how is it with the bad dreams?" he asked softly. "Was Talking River successful in driving the bad dreams from you?"

"Yes," I answered truthfully, "the nightmares with monster creatures are no longer. But still I dream, Five Killer, and in my dreams I see a small child who cries out for her mother." I twisted around so I could look into his eyes. "What of my other family, Five Killer? You were the one who found me sitting by the river. Did you ask anyone about my family? Perhaps my mother is still alive; perhaps I have brothers or sisters."

His eyes shifted from mine and searched the mountains in the distance before he made his answer. Gently he stroked my hair. "A few survived. An old man was found hiding in his asi. I think he no longer lives today. And a young man with a small son survived—I don't remember his name—but he was not of your family. No one else remained."

"Perhaps some of my family escaped to the surrounding villages," I persisted.

"No, Dancing Leaf, it is not so."

"What of the village? Surely someone returned to the area, and surely the town was rebuilt."

"No Cherokee towns exist where your village once was. Now the land belongs to the white man," he said, and I heard bitterness in his voice. He unwrapped himself from me and walked to the water's edge. "We should never have fought with Jackson against the Creeks."

"With Jackson, the American warrior?" I asked. "You mean we fought with Americans against a neighbor tribe?" The Cherokees and Creeks had long had border wars of their own, but surely two Indian nations would have fought as brothers against the white man.

Five Killer bent down, picked up a rock, and marked an X on the ground. "Your village, High Water, was located in the low country on the banks of the Coowassee River." He made wavy lines to show the river. "Across the river," he said, making several X's to designate Creek villages, "was the land of the Creeks."

He sat down and stared at his drawings before speaking again. "Now I am ashamed. Many of our great leaders served in Jackson's army—

Ridge, Junaluska, White Path, Going Snake, Charles Hicks. We defeated the Creek, but hundreds of men died on both sides. And the white soldiers, returning to their homelands, showed their gratitude by taking what they wanted from Cherokee farms—horses, pigs, cattle. Jackson denied it, even when Ridge confronted him."

"But my village was a Cherokee village. Why would the Unaka soldiers destroy a Cherokee town?"

"Ah, yes, of course you lived in a Cherokee village, but it was close to the Creek boundary line, and many of the people in your village were friendly with the Creeks. When Creek warriors took refuge in High Water, the white soldiers thought the village belonged to the Creeks. And so your village was burned and the people killed, and this also Jackson would not admit."

"They thought we were Creeks?" I repeated.

"Yes, or so they said. Many Unakas do not see Cherokees or Creeks. They only see Indians."

Five Killer did not often talk of bad times. When others complained about the wickedness of the whites, he was silent or instead would tell an amusing story that turned everyone's attention. And he did not dwell on these distressing thoughts now, for he grabbed me off the rock and twirled me around and said, "And so that is how Dancing Leaf came to live with us, and that is how in my mid-life I came to have a beautiful little sister to tease and throw in the river." He walked with me wrapped tightly in his arms to the water's edge, but then he allowed me to squirm free from his grasp. "And now she is too strong for me." His eyes looked me up and down as he said that. "I would race you to the house, but my legs are old and tired."

"Yes," I replied, as I strode forward, pretending to leave him behind. "You are now an old man, and I am glad that you have Raven to look after you and that I don't have to do so." I stopped, though, and reached for his hand and was glad to have had this time with Five Killer.

But the memories that had rushed to me with the running water were not so easily dismissed. Before we reached the cabin, a thought came to me and I knew what I must do.

"The Cherokee council meets near Major Ridge's home in half a moon's time," I said to Five Killer. "I will go to this council meeting. People from all parts of the Cherokee nation will be there. I will ask if anyone knows of survivors from my village. Then, if no one answers, then I will be sure."

Five Killer sighed a long sigh and then frowned.

"You will take me?" I asked.

"You are a very stubborn one," he replied, but he did not sound angry as he said it, nor did he answer my question. He simply squeezed my hand, and we went into the cabin together.

The babies had fallen asleep on the bear rugs, and while everyone else settled into their rooms, I took Chera to the barn so she could feed her puppies. They nursed frantically at first, and I thought perhaps I had kept Chera with me too long. But when their round bellies were full and they lay still against each other, I called Chera to follow me. I wanted her to sleep near me on my first night back.

The glow of the moon was bright, and we easily made our way along the path. As we passed the garden, I saw a raccoon, who sat up and looked at me with no fear. When Chera charged at him, he backed away and lazily waddled off to the woods. I wished I had brought Long Fellow's gun, for that would have scared him off, or perhaps, if I shot straight, we could have coon stew tomorrow, although I had never killed an animal before.

The earth crumbled under my feet as I made my way between the rows of vegetables. The pumpkin vines were dried and withered, as well as the potato tops. I reached down and dug one potato out; it was small and scraggly. The next day, in daylight, I would have to judge whether to leave the potatoes in the ground or begin pulling up the early ones.

Five Killer was talking with Long Fellow on the porch when we returned. Five Killer held a lantern in one hand and a paper in the other. "I almost forgot," he said, addressing me. "Major Ridge has sent word that he is coming to inspect our building in two days. It seems that Jonathan and members of his church have written asking that the inn be used as a mission church for Sunday services. He wants to discuss this matter with us to see if we approve, and then he will make a recommendation to the council meeting."

I was surprised by such news. How was it that Jonathan would counsel with our own head chief? But my thoughts were interrupted when Five Killer handed me the paper. "Ridge's daughter Nancy has sent you this letter," he said.

"Perhaps Nancy will come with him," I said excitedly as I unfolded it.

Dearest Dancing Leaf,

Much has happened. I have heard about Beloved Mother's death, and my heart has grieved for you. I, too, did not return to the mission school, but have married, and now I am with child. My time is soon come. Return with my father and visit with me. I am lonely for our talks. Perhaps when you arrive, my new one will be with us. You can help to take care of him. I hope you will come.

Your true friend,
Nancy Ridge

"She wants me to return with her father for a visit," I said to Five Killer. I did not know if I was ready to travel in a new direction so soon. I had just come home.

But Raven's voice came from the shadows behind us. "It will be good for you to go," she said, stepping into view. "You can see how a young bride lives. Besides, the Ridges are powerful people, and you will benefit from such good company."

Perhaps I will go, but I will take no counsel from you! Those words were in my head, but I said nothing and quietly unrolled my mat and Long Fellow's, too, so that we could begin our sleep. Soon the muffled voices of the others quieted, and I knew all had gone to bed. I was glad for the cool breeze because our bodies were still moist with the heat of the day.

Nancy Ridge was my best friend at the mission school even though she was several years older. I often thought of her as a sister. The school had no sleeping room for girls, so in the evenings we stayed with Mrs. Vann, the Cherokee widow of Chief Vann. We had a cat then. We called her Snow because she was pure white. The old Cherokees

80

believed cats brought bad fortune, and they would not let their children have them. So we let Snow in by the window every evening, and out she went every morning. Mrs. Vann said nothing about the short white hairs on the covers; perhaps she liked cats.

With such thoughts I drifted into a peaceful sleep, but before long I was jolted awake and saw Long Fellow sitting up and Chera standing with her ears pricked forward.

"What's wrong?" I whispered.

"Coyotes," Long Fellow said softly. "They're too close."

I sat up and listened to the howling in the distance. I thought I heard more than one, but I couldn't judge how many.

"Did you shut the barn door?" Long Fellow asked.

"I did."

"A coyote loves nothing better than a black speckled hen."

I do not know how long we listened, but soon I was asleep once again. I awoke to the gray of early morning. I quickly pulled my feet under me and sat up and strained as I listened carefully. Something was wrong, and I was sure this was no matter from my dream world. The birds above chattered in a noisy clamor, and a squirrel barked from the oak tree on the side of the cabin.

Cautiously I walked down the steps of the cabin. Then I heard a bawl from Rosie, followed by loud thumping as if she might be trying to get out of her stall. Chera charged toward the barn and barked furiously at the doorway until I reached it. When I turned the block of wood and pulled the door open, Chera bolted like a streak of lightning, her eyes catching what I could not.

My eyes were slow to adjust to the dimness, and I gasped when I saw the figure of a coyote scooting under a dug-out place in the back of the barn. Chera charged toward him but then promptly turned to another coyote who had been standing in the shadows and who now rushed past me, out the open door. I saw that this coyote had something in his mouth, and it was not a speckled hen, but a small, mewling puppy. Chera was at his heels, her bark a raging bark.

I followed behind, screaming as loudly as I could, but both the coyote and Chera were well into the distance. I ran back, slid a bridle into

Red Sky's mouth, and urged her up the hillside. When we reached the top, I thought about the rifle I should have brought with me.

On the other side of the hill, I saw the two figures in battle. Chera and the coyote were one large ball of fur rolling over the ground. I could not tell where one stopped and where the other began amongst the snarling sounds and yelps and squirting blood.

The first coyote lurked nearby, eyeing me suspiciously as I approached, and then in one swift motion he grabbed something from the ground. Only then did I realize it was the red puppy. As he ran into the brush, I climbed down from Red Sky and charged toward Chera and the fighting coyote, screaming and shaking my fist. And soon enough the action stopped, but then Chera was lying on the ground and the coyote was standing. He did not turn to look at me but darted into the thickness of the brush.

I kneeled beside Chera. She whimpered as my hand touched her head. I thought she could not move, so I sat beside her, soothing her with soft words and gently stroking her back. A shudder went from her head to her tail, and then she was totally still, and I knew the breath of life had left her.

THE DAUGHTER OF THE SUN

At one time Sun hated the people of earth because they could never look at her without squinting and frowning. "My grandchildren are so ugly," she told her brother Moon.

"I think they are quite handsome," Moon disagreed. The earth children always smiled when they looked up at him.

Sun was so jealous that she sent down scorching rays. This caused a great fever, and many earth men died.

The Little People agreed to help the earth children take revenge on the sun. They knew that Sun visited her daughter every day, midway across the sky vault, so they sent a rattlesnake, who coiled beside the door, eagerly waiting for Sun to depart. When the daughter opened the door, the snake sprang up and bit the daughter, and she fell immediately. So the daughter was killed and not Sun, and the rattlesnake fled in terror.

When Sun realized her daughter was dead, she went inside and grieved, and a period of great darkness followed. The earth children went to the Little People again, who told them they would have to bring back Sun's daughter from the ghost country. Seven men traveled to the ghost country, where they found the young woman. They struck her with a rod and put her in a box. They knew they must not open the box, no matter what occurred, for that is what the Little People had instructed.

The girl came quickly to life and called out to them, but they ignored her. First she asked for food, then she asked for water. Finally she begged for them to raise the lid a little, for she was smothering. This time they lifted the lid just a small space to give her some air. But when they did, they heard a fluttering sound, and something flew past them into the thicket. When they reached the settlement and opened the box, nothing was inside.

Now, if the men had kept the box closed, they could have brought the daughter back safely from the land of the dead, and we could all bring back friends and loved ones from the ghost country. But since they did not, we will never be able to bring back the dead to the land of the living.

Chapter 7

Jonathan Young was the first to come upon Chera and me. I was sitting under a pine tree, singing the death song and rocking back and forth with Chera in my arms.

> She is gone, O Great One;
> May her soul rise to the first heaven, the tops of the trees;
> Let her soul ascend to the second heaven, among the clouds;
> May her soul move on to the third heaven, as high as the moon;
> Let her soul fly to the fourth heaven, next to the bright, warm sun;
> May her soul climb to the fifth heaven, mingling with distant stars;
> Let her soul be in the sixth heaven, where the constellations live;
> May her soul rest at the seventh heaven in Galunlati, the home of
>   the Great Creator.

I sang the song over and over until the rays of the sun were at a blinding slant, and then I looked up and noticed Jonathan watching me.

"Dancing Leaf," he began softly, "what happened?"

I told him with stumbling words about Chera's brave fight with the coyotes. "I have caused this," I said. "Chera should have been in the barn with her two puppies, but I wanted her with me. If she had been in the barn, the coyotes would never have tried to enter."

Jonathan bent down and let his gaze fall on Chera in my arms.

"If I had taken a gun with me," I continued, "I could have shot them or scared them off." I shook my head in disgust. "I hate coyotes."

"It's not your fault, Dancing Leaf," he said gently, placing his hand on my shoulder. "Come on," he urged. "We will take her back and bury her."

"Will you kill the coyote?"

"Yes," he agreed, but his voice held no anger or hatred. "Tonight. I'll get him, Dancing Leaf."

He helped me to my feet, but I would not give him Chera, whom I kept locked in my arms. Then he boosted me onto my horse, and he climbed on behind, and slowly we made our way down the hill to the cabin.

Five Killer and Long Fellow were on the porch waiting, and their eyes shifted from the bundle that was Chera to my face, as I slowly dismounted and walked toward them.

"Damn coyotes!" Five Killer muttered.

"The heat has driven the animal world mad," Long Fellow said in his low voice. He turned and went inside the cabin, and I knew he would lie down on his mat and close his eyes, even though the morning was still young.

"We will bury her by the creek," I announced.

"I don't know, Dancing Leaf," Five Killer counseled gently. "The animals go there to drink, and one will surely dig her up. It would be better to bury her in a dry spot."

"We will put a mound of stones on top." I began the descent to the creek.

Jonathan was soon behind me with a shovel, and he dug a knee-deep grave. We had no burial box, so I wrapped Chera in a blue blanket. Jonathan tenderly placed her in the open womb of earth. I watched as he filled it with dirt again. We walked along the creek and chose the larger stones, which we mounded on top of the grave.

"Thank you, Jonathan," I said simply as we placed the last stone— a large gray one that glittered with gold streaks.

He rested against the shovel for a moment, his breaths long and hard, small streams running down the sides of his face. He leaned toward me and said, "Come back with me now. Turtle Woman will fix you something to eat."

I shook my head. "Tell the others I am in mourning and do not wish to be disturbed."

"Dancing Leaf," he entreated, his voice soft and even—I could not help but look at him, because although he had said my name many times before, it was as if he were saying it then for the very first time—"I am sad about Chera, too, but animals don't have souls, and it's not proper to mourn them the way you do a person."

Ai-yee! He had been so kind, and I had felt our hearts were together, but at these words, my heart turned to stone. I opened my mouth, but then I shut it because I did not wish to taint this sacred time with words of anger. So I said nothing, but I folded my face into my body and remained in this position until I heard his footsteps leaving.

I then stretched out upon Grandfather Rock and looked above at the canopy of gently dancing leaves provided by the tall sycamore tree. The tree was so large, and the leaves so dense, that the sun's scorching rays could not penetrate. I closed my eyes and thought of Raven, who was surely scolding me from afar because I wasn't helping with the chores or the children, but it mattered not to me. I heard the sounds of axes and hammers on fallen trees, and I knew the men were working on the inn. Voices called back and forth to each other, but I could not understand what they said.

A picture of Beloved Mother came to mind. She was only eighteen years of age when she sat by the stream, rigid and still, mourning the death of her first husband, Kingfisher. For three days she barely moved from that spot until she was assured in a vision that he had risen to the seventh heaven.

Jonathan's words returned to me: *Animals do not have souls, Dancing Leaf.* I sat up and spit into the stream to remove the bitter taste from my mouth.

Chera's lost puppy appeared to me then, and my heart grieved anew, so I sang for her the song of seven heavens, and I sang it seven times and was glad that I had thought to do so.

At sunset Jonathan approached once more, and he brought a bowl of corn chowder and two strips of deer meat. I shook my head, for still I could not think of food.

"There's still the one puppy left—the speckled one," he reminded me. "I've been letting him lick cow's milk from my finger today, but it won't be enough. I'll take him back to town with me," he offered. "I know a fellow who has a bitch with a small litter. Maybe the mother dog will let this one nurse."

"That would be good." I had forgotten about the remaining puppy, and I realized that I wished that it had been the girl puppy, the one who resembled Chera, who had survived. But no, it was the speckled male. "I'm glad you have thought of him," I said, slowly turning to Jonathan.

He placed the bowl of chowder on the ground and then stepped behind me and straddled the rock, so that my back was to him. His arms encircled mine, and I let myself rest against his chest. I felt the steady beat of his heart, and I liked feeling safe and protected in this way, but suddenly I remembered the last night that Blue Lake and I had sat on this rock. A jolting thought came to me, and I said it aloud: "What will Blue Lake think when he learns Chera has died in my care?"

"He'll understand," Jonathan answered, and his lips brushed the top of my head.

We remained on the rock for a long while, until I was sure that Raven would be tired herself and would not make demands of me, and then we walked hand in hand back to the cabin.

At nightfall, I took my sleeping mat out onto the porch again, and Jonathan unrolled his blanket and stretched out there, too. When we heard the howl of coyotes, he quickly rose to his feet, taking his gun.

I heard two shots from the upper ridge, and I heard the coyotes no more that night. Jonathan was gone the next morning when I awoke.

"He has taken the puppy back to town," Five Killer informed me, "to suckle with the mother dog."

I was relieved that Jonathan had thought of this.

"Remember," Five Killer added, "today is the day Major Ridge will come to inspect the new inn."

I thought of Nancy, whom I wanted to see with all of my heart, but I did not feel ready to travel away from home yet.

At midmorning Jonathan returned, so excited with his news, that his words rushed forward like a mountain stream after a storm. "He latched right on, Dancing Leaf," he said of the speckled pup. "And the mother acted like he'd been there the whole time. I wish you could have seen it."

"It is good news." My own voice was flat and calm like a mountain lake. I should have cared more about the speckled pup, but I could not; I was glad Jonathan did.

"The Darbys are a real nice family, Dancing Leaf. They don't mind a bit. They said you can have him back as soon as he is weaned."

I forced a smile and reached forward and lightly squeezed his hand.

The day passed in the usual manner. I milked the cow. I pulled weeds from the garden and dug ripe potatoes from the ground. When I put them in the storage shed, I noticed the pile was small, compared to the past year. If the rains did not come soon, we would not have enough for the coming winter.

By late afternoon Major Ridge still had not arrived, and so I sat down with my pen and paper at the table while the babies napped.

"What is it you write?" Raven asked.

I did not look up as my pen moved across the paper. "I am informing Blue Lake of the death of Chera."

She made a sound, as if a fly had landed on her nose. "Blue Lake has another life with his new family. He doesn't care about this old life now."

The pen fell from my hand, and my eyes flew to her face, because her words stung so sharply. But I regretted immediately that she saw my pain, and I quickly lowered my gaze, retrieved the pen, and resumed writing. "Still, Chera was his dog, and he should know," I answered, keeping my voice even.

"Well, listen to me, Dancing Leaf." Raven sat down next to me. "Your sad heart and your grieving ways drove him away," she lectured. "And they will drive off Jonathan, too, if you continue in this manner. You must think of your future."

Carefully I placed the pen on the table. I turned toward the window; I would not look at Raven.

Surely, she knew her words were poison darts, but still she persisted. "I know I speak harshly to you, Dancing Leaf, but I do so as a mother, since you have none. It is time you married and began a family of your own. You cannot stay here forever."

A rancid taste, like the taste of the bitter fern leaf, formed in my mouth. I did not spit, as I would have liked to, but the bitterness came out in my words: "Thank you for your great kindness, Mother." I rose and gathered my writing things and put them in the pouch and took them with me to the rock, where it was not so easy to write, but at least I could gather thoughts quietly.

"Blue Lake," I began. "I hope that you have arrived safely at your father's home. I must inform you of sad news." I wrote the story of Chera's death and told how bravely she had fought. I apologized for not taking good care of my charge.

I reread the words and was folding the paper before the tears in my eyes could spill over and smudge the ink, when I felt a presence behind me. I was surprised to see Long Fellow, who still moves lightly on his feet, even though his knee does not bend.

He leaned down and carefully studied the paper, even though he cannot read. "You have not written enough," he said. When my eyes searched his for more meaning, he added, "You must tell him what is in your heart."

"I know of no heart matters," I retorted, because the thought came to my mind again that Blue Lake could have invited me to travel with him.

This time Long Fellow made the sound of a snorting horse.

"Tell him about the inn." Five Killer, who was now standing beside Long Fellow, said these words. "About how we are rebuilding to make it a place of business. Soon many traveling people will stop, and these people will buy goods. We could use a fine mind like his to do the numbers and writing. If he wishes to return, there is much he can do."

"I will write your message," I said. "But I can do numbers and write, too, Five Killer."

"Ah, yes, that is true, Dancing Leaf."

But I knew his thoughts. He would prefer to have another man in the household. There were already too many women.

I wrote Five Killer's words, exactly as he had said them, assuring

Blue Lake that these were Five Killer's thoughts. Long Fellow and Five Killer headed back to the cabin, but when they were halfway up the hill, Long Fellow looked back at me and I knew that he hoped I was writing more.

Long Fellow was right about most things. Why should I not tell Blue Lake the thoughts of my heart? The words began to flow in my mind, and I let my pen record them on the page. I briefly described Talking River, the adawehi in Coosa Town. I told Blue Lake about the dreams that were cured and the dreams that still came. The crystal, I assured him, was safely in my medicine pouch, and I explained how Spider Woman and I had purified it. I hoped he was finding his truth path, I added, and said that I, too, was searching for my own.

I put the pen down and read the letter from top to bottom. I thought it a very fine letter and began to fold it, when the words of Long Fellow once more echoed in my mind: *Tell him what is in your heart.* I unfolded the letter, picked up the pen, and wrote, "I hope that our two paths will meet again soon." And then I put the letter in the pouch and rode Red Sky to town.

I left the letter with the white agent, where it would be picked up and carried east by the horseman. When I returned, still Ridge had not come. Nor did he come on the second or third day.

On the fourth day, a messenger arrived saying Major Ridge had been delayed and it would be several more days before he could travel. Finally, on the tenth day, the twins came running in from the porch, jumping up and down, pointing outside, and talking in their jumbled words.

"What are they saying?" Raven asked.

"They are talking about a big, black bug," I answered, and we went to see what menace they were describing.

We laughed when we saw it, for approaching in the distance was a black carriage with large, round wheels. Excitedly, I ran down the steps. I knew it belonged to Major Ridge because often he had driven it to the mission school with his wife to visit Nancy and her brother, John. When the carriage was close enough, I saw John's face appear in the window. Benjamin, their black slave, sat on the top bench, holding the reins of the horse. He stopped the coach in front of the porch, and John exited. I peered inside and saw the red velvet seats, but there was no one else.

A full year had passed since I last saw John Ridge. He was now taller and thinner, his face longer, and his dark eyes larger in his face than before; his hair was cut short, and he was dressed not in Cherokee clothes, but in white man's clothes with breeches, a shirt with ruffles, and a dark coat.

He was handsome, yet not so handsome as Blue Lake. He and Blue Lake were good friends, and often I had compared them. I preferred Blue Lake's gentle spirit. John often argued with our teachers; Blue Lake would only disagree in his mind.

When the Gambolds, our teachers at the mission school, had lectured us on the evils of the ball play and dancing, John declared nothing was wrong with either. Later that evening he organized a ball game with the other boys, and they stripped down to their loincloths and played for several hours. Mother Gambold urged John to be baptized and saved by Jesus, who would make his heart pure. John informed her that perhaps the white world needed to be saved, but the red world did not, for all Cherokee were assured of rising to the seventh heaven if they followed the path of peace.

So it surprised me now to see that he looked so much like a person of the white world.

"Dancing Leaf, how good to see you," he began, his voice rounder and deeper than I remembered.

He took my hand in his, and I curtsied as I was taught at the mission school. No smile appeared on his face, though, and his eyes had the look of one who had not slept for several nights.

My manners were pushed aside by my questions. "John, what is wrong? You have come to tell me bad news, haven't you?"

"Perhaps we could sit down," he replied.

"Yes, yes," I agreed. "Come in. We will have something to eat and drink. Tell Benjamin to unhitch the horse and fetch water for him from the well. He can tie him under the trees to the west of the cabin to rest and graze."

We were soon up the small steps and standing on the porch. I introduced both Turtle and Raven. Raven, I could see, was impressed with this young brave.

"We are pleased to have you as a guest," she assured John. "And your father will be coming soon also?" Raven had already made mention to her friends in town that the prominent Major Ridge was to visit our home.

"Not at this time," he answered. "A grave circumstance prevents his coming. I have come to speak to Dancing Leaf about it."

"You must tell us of this serious matter," Raven entreated, her voice light and sweet. "We will do all we can to help."

Have you no manners? You can see that he wants to speak to me—alone! Those words charged through my mind, but I swallowed them and instead spoke gently, my own voice light and sweet. "Raven, perhaps you could bring us refreshments. John is surely tired and thirsty after the long ride." I smiled pleasantly, as if I knew she would be happy to do this.

Of course, she wasn't, and she stood with her mouth open because she would have preferred that I bring refreshments.

But Turtle was beside her and quick to respond. "Yes, yes, Mother. We will bring our guest some refreshment while he visits with Dancing Leaf."

Still Raven stood uncertainly until Turtle linked her arm through Raven's and with some effort forced her toward the door.

"You are not well?" I asked when the two of them were inside and we had seated ourselves. "Is it your hip that bothers you?"

"No! No!" he exclaimed, and I regretted that I had mentioned it, because he was always embarrassed by his deformity. The doctors declared it a "scrofulous" condition of the hip that caused him to walk with a limp. I, of course, had never seen this hip, but Blue Lake said that it turned red and was swollen and so painful that sometimes John could not stand or walk.

"My hip is doing well at this time, but I must tell you bad news." He turned to me, but his eyes were lost in a gaze that went to a place beyond my face. And then his words tumbled out. "Nancy has died. It has been a week now. She was in childbirth; it was a difficult time for her. She did not survive."

I gasped, and because he had spoken so quickly, I repeated the words several times in my own mind. Desperately, I wanted to believe that I had heard wrong. "Oh, no," I protested. "Surely, it cannot be. Not Nancy. No, not Nancy!"

He slowly nodded.

The pain I felt was too great for sitting, and I rose and walked the length of the porch back and forth several times. I leaned against the railing for a moment to steady myself, and then I walked the distance once more. A stern voice in my head said, *You must comfort this grieving brother,* but the same sadness that stilled my tongue when my mother was lost and when Beloved Mother died and when Chera was killed silenced me now. I did not stand in silence alone, though, for John rose and put his arms around me. I buried my face in his shoulder, and tears streamed from both of us.

"Dancing Leaf . . . I am sorry to bring you this sad news."

And then my voice returned, and my manners also. I drew back and spoke. "Forgive me. Your grief is larger than my own. I should be comforting you."

The door opened, and Raven emerged with a plate of bread smeared with raspberry jam. John and I parted and resumed our seated positions.

"Thank you, Raven," I said mildly, and I could see many things on her face as she presented each of us a square of bread.

Turtle gave us a glass of sweet tea, and I was grateful to her when she said, "Come, Mother, these two have matters they must discuss alone."

John ate his bread, but I was not hungry and insisted that he have mine. He ate all of mine and even took another one from the plate.

"I am sorry you have lost your sister, John. I am sorry that your parents have lost their daughter. I do not know her husband, but I am sorry that he has lost his bride. I am sorry to have lost such a friend. What of the baby?"

John shook his head. "He did not live."

The porch was well shaded, and a gentle breeze lifted the ruffles of my skirt, but still, the heat of midday was thick about us. My forehead was damp with sweat. I lifted my braids to cool my neck, and John removed his jacket and laid it on the back of the chair.

We sat in silence for a while longer until Five Killer appeared and said immediately, "I am sorry to hear of the death of your sister." And then I knew that Raven had been listening at the door.

"Thank you, Five Killer," John said. "It is good to see you. My father sends his regrets that he will not be able to come at this time and help with the decision about the mission church. He will come at a later time."

"No matter. We grieve with him over the loss of his daughter."

Silence descended again, and Five Killer lowered himself to the floor and sat beside us. We watched as a red-tailed hawk circled the meadow. I held my breath to see if he would dive for prey. Perhaps he was full and satisfied and was simply enjoying the sun and sky, for he soared back to a dead tree limb and perched there, quietly surveying his domain.

"Father asks if Dancing Leaf would return with me," John began. "Mother was pleased when Nancy invited her to visit, and now she wishes that Dancing Leaf would come and attend the graveside service. Her presence would be a comfort to both of my parents." He spoke to Five Killer as if he were asking permission of a father, but Five Killer turned his gaze to me.

I thought of the Ridges' home. I had visited there several times, and Susanna and Major Ridge were always kind, treating me like a daughter, but I did not feel ready to travel so soon.

When Five Killer saw my hesitation, he quickly reminded me, "Dancing Leaf, you want to attend the council meeting. It would be easy enough to travel with John and visit with the family, then you can all proceed to the meeting, which will be held on ground nearby."

"Will you come, Dancing Leaf?" John asked.

I saw the earnestness in John Ridge's eyes, and I felt the sorrow of his mother and father. And what Five Killer said was true—the council grounds were near the Ridges' home.

"Yes, yes, I will go with you," I answered, and there was no longer any question.

"How are things with Blue Lake?" John inquired of Five Killer. "He did not return to the mission school last year. Is he still with you?"

I answered before Five Killer could. "He has gone to visit his white father in Virginia."

"Oh." John's eyes rested on me, but I would not return his look.

We had a few more moments of quiet before Raven burst in upon us. She offered words of consolation and then turned the talk to other things. "What fine clothes you wear, John. Does your mother make them?"

"Not anymore. My mother finds pictures in the books at the white men's stores. Our slaves make them from material we order from Charleston."

"You must see my spinning wheel," Raven offered, "and the many things I have made. But first I must see this coach of yours. How fine and beautiful it is, and there is even a roof so you are protected from sun and rain. Come and show me this carriage."

The two of them went on a small journey in the carriage and returned to observe the brightly colored scarves and sashes Raven stored inside a trunk. She insisted that John take a red turban, because it contrasted well with the black of his suit, and we all admired it when he wound it around his head.

"I must apologize for these scars on my arm," Raven ventured. "Surely they offend you even to look at them."

"I had noticed them, but nothing offends me when I look at you, Raven." John glanced at Five Killer, who immediately put an arm around Raven.

She slowly ran her fingers along the pink scars. "Perhaps Dancing Leaf should tell you how I came by them."

My eyes grew wide at this, because surely she would be embarrassing me by complaining of how I insisted that we rest in the very path of a bear. But she spoke again before I could say anything.

"No, I think Dancing Leaf is too modest. I will tell the story myself." She leaned forward and extended her arm so John could have a closer view of the long scars. "I could have lost my life if it had not been for Dancing Leaf, for the large she-bear swung forward with her powerful arm. I fell backwards, so only the tips of her claws tore through me. But her next assault would have taken off my head if Dancing Leaf had not charged forward, throwing rocks, calling out a challenge that made the bear stop."

Such words of praise to come from Raven! Of course, the reason was made clear later when she helped me pack my things. "Perhaps the major and his wife wish to find a bride for their handsome son," she counseled. "I have been busy all day, making this new blue skirt for you, and I will give you this calico one of mine also. I hardly wear it. It goes well with this white cotton blouse. Your old clothes are not proper for a visit."

I turned my eyes skyward, and Beloved Mother's counsel came to me: *There are times to make good use of a thunder being.* Finally, I was having such a time. Although I did not wish to owe Raven favors, I was excited to have new clothes. Turtle plaited my hair, weaving ribbons of red and blue throughout as she did so.

"Dancing Leaf, you must take more care with your appearance from now on," Raven advised. "See what a beautiful maiden she is when we have properly dressed her?" she remarked to Turtle, as if I were not there.

"It is a time of grieving," I reminded her. I knew in my heart that John had many things to accomplish before he put his thoughts to marriage, and he had never showed an interest in me; it was his cousin, Buck Watie, who often flirted and teased me at the mission school.

"Yes, there will be grieving," Raven said. "So you must take your time; there is no need to hurry. Things are crowded here, anyway. Stay and be of help to these people. The major is a very important man. Many young braves visit his home daily, no doubt."

Although this talk did not please me, I knew I must press my advantage, so I dared not scowl or make sad faces. Instead, my words were grateful ones. "Thank you, Raven! The clothes are lovely. You are so kind."

And so Raven fetched another skirt, a striped one, and also two sashes—a red one and a blue one to wear around my waist.

When we were seated at our evening meal, I realized that Jonathan had already left for his home, although he often took his evening meal with us. I wondered how he felt about the presence of John Ridge and was sorry that I would not see him before I left.

There was much talk throughout the meal about Major Ridge, for Five Killer had known him many years.

"Do you know how your father acquired his name?" he asked John.

"I have been told that at one time he had another name, Pathkiller, because he had once slain the enemy in the path."

"Yes," Five Killer continued, "he was a great warrior in his youth, but after he married and settled down with children, he was called 'Ridge,' because he was often seen walking along the ridge of the mountaintop when he was out hunting." Five Killer spoke of Major Ridge's fearlessness as he led Cherokee forces at the Battle of Horseshoe Bend. "Although," he added, "perhaps he has come to regret that time, like I have, because we fought against the Creeks."

"Of one thing he is not proud," John asserted. "He killed a Cherokee man many years ago, and the deed still haunts him."

"Yes, it was Doublehead," Five Killer informed us. "Your father did the tribe a great favor by getting rid of such an evil man."

"Who was Doublehead?" I asked, vaguely recalling mention of him from days gone by.

Five Killer began the story. "Doublehead was at one time a great chief and warrior, but in later years he had no heart. He killed white men and roasted their bodies and ate of them."

I gasped at this thought. How could any man of any race commit such a horrible deed?

"His greatest crimes were against his own people," Five Killer continued. "As a Cherokee chief, he made treaties with the whites, accepting their bribes, so that with each treaty, his own wealth doubled. He owned many slaves and had much land."

"That, in my opinion," John inserted, "has been one of our greatest failures in dealing with the white world. We have too many chiefs in too many places, and we have not spoken with one voice."

I looked at John with new interest when he spoke. These were no longer the words of a schoolboy angry with his schoolmaster. They were the words of a statesman, a man of learning.

"It will not be like that in the future," he continued. "We will have one government like the white world and one elected chief who speaks for us. And no decisions will be made unless by agreement of the council."

I liked hearing his words. I liked that John's mind was on such things. My own thoughts were too crowded with my own concerns. *Where will I go? Where will be my home? Whom will I marry? Will our crops last through the dry summer?* I had given little thought to the larger issues of the welfare of our tribe.

"But tell me more about this Doublehead," John prodded. "My father would not tell the story."

"Doublehead's greatest crime," Five Killer explained, "was taken against his own wife, who was a sister of Vann's wife. He killed the baby in her womb and beat this wife until she was dead."

Again I gasped, placing my hand over my heart. I could hardly believe that any man would kill his own wife and baby.

"Chief Vann," Five Killer added, "would not allow such a thing and claimed the right of revenge according to the clan laws. In the old days, a clansman must avenge a wrongful death."

"So Chief Vann killed Doublehead?" John asked.

"Doublehead was not an easy man to kill." Five Killer sat back and lit his pipe. The story was not a simple one. "Vann was a man who liked to drink, and he overdrank on the night the deed was to be committed, and so the task was left to your father. Ridge found Doublehead seated in a tavern and shot him directly and then fled. But the bullet went through his jaw without killing him, and so Ridge asked Saunders, a friend, to help him. The next night, they found him recuperating in a farmer's loft. They fired on him again, but Doublehead lunged forward, and he and Ridge struggled, fighting with knives, hand to hand, until finally Saunders sunk his hatchet into Doublehead's skull."

Ai-yee! I was glad that Doublehead had been brought to justice. But in such a bloody manner! The talk was too much for me, although I was glad Five Killer ended the story with words of assurance: "Your father did our people a great favor by killing this evil man."

I wished to hear no more of this talk, however. Turtle had left long ago to attend to the children, and Raven had excused herself after we cleared the table, so I was the only woman still present. The food from my meal was not resting in my stomach, but swirling about dangerously, so I quickly bid everyone good-night and walked about in the fresh evening air while the men continued their discussion. They talked on, as men love to do when wine is on the table and their pipes are lit; they talked for several hours more.

I took my sleeping mat and Long Fellow's to the porch and stretched them out, although I knew Long Fellow would not retire until the others did. I was alone with my thoughts, but I would not dwell on death and violence. Instead, I chose to think about the happier days when Nancy and I were friends at the mission school.

I remembered how we laughed and told stories late into the night. Sometimes we hid cookies and other treats in our skirts, and when we were sure Mrs. Vann was asleep, we would spread our assortment on the bed for a midwinter picnic. We let the white cat, Snow, in through the window so she could share our party. One time in late September, when the weather was still warm, we snuck out and went swimming in the creek. Of course, we had to remove our clothes. We were being very quiet, enjoying the cool water under the early autumn moon, when suddenly we heard branches rustling and footsteps approaching. We never knew who was there, but we were back into our clothes and then back in bed, breathing heavily, and too afraid to sleep the rest of the night. Nancy thought we had heard the ghost of Chief Vann himself.

I could not keep the sad thoughts from stealing into my mind then. Why did evil people such as Doublehead exist? To kill one's own wife and baby—there could be no greater crime. It was even worse than the crime of the coyote who stole puppies from the mother dog. And what of Nancy? She had a loving father and family to protect and care for her, and still she died a painful death.

Mothers and babies, babies and mothers—the thoughts and images crowded my mind, demanding my attention. Mothers and babies should not die. Nor should they be parted by death. At least Nancy was with her baby in the Upper Worlds, and Chera rested there, too, with

HOW THE REDBIRD GOT HIS COLOR

Little Bird was a small bird who wanted to be noticed and respected like the sacred eagle. He was such a plain, earth-colored bird, however, he was scarcely visible in the natural world. Perhaps if he were red, he mused, others would admire his power and beauty, especially the female birds.

An elder explained to him that red was a sacred color and would have to be earned in a special way with the help of a vision. Little Bird waited, but no vision came.

One day he was caught in the middle of Raccoon and Wolf's game. Now, Raccoon was tired of Wolf's tricks, so he challenged Wolf to a race to the river. Raccoon raced forward and grabbed hold of a yellow root on the bank. Wolf came after him but could not stop in time and charged headlong into the rapids.

Wolf hated cold water, and he could not swim, so he cried out to Raccoon for help. Raccoon ignored him. Somehow Wolf made it to the clay bank. Exhausted, he fell into a deep sleep. Raccoon snuck out then and packed damp, red clay on Wolf's eyes. The clay hardened by the time Wolf awoke.

Little Bird heard Wolf's cries. "Help me! Help me! I can't see! Please help!"

"I will help," Little Bird said, "but you must promise to play nicely and not torture Raccoon with your many tricks."

Wolf agreed and even promised to tell Little Bird where he could get red color if he would help. So Little Bird pecked at the clay until it all fell off. Wolf showed the bird a plant called Red Paint Brush that would allow Little Bird to paint himself red.

To this day, Wolf plays fairly with Raccoon, and Little Bird is now Redbird, a bird of fine distinction.

Chapter 8

With the presence of John Ridge and his slave Benjamin, the cabin was even more crowded. Raven moved in with Turtle and the twins. Five Killer gave his sleeping place to John and retired to the porch with Long Fellow and me, and then Five Killer himself heard the rumbling of Long Fellow's snores.

"See, I told you," I said. "His snoring is so loud, it drives the varmints from the garden." Without Chera to chase them, I had worried that night creatures would raid the garden, so I slept with the gun by my side. But one night when I rose to shoot, Long Fellow suddenly went through a loud series of snorts and snores, and two creatures scampered back to the woods.

Raven arose early the next morning to see John and me off. Instead of her usual calico dress, she wore a green one made of cloth that glistened in the morning light. She set large bowls of simmered squirrel meat before us. "I told Five Killer these young people would need a substantial meal to begin such a journey," she said, "and so he himself was up early to shoot the squirrel. And I have packed a meal with roasted venison. Your slave has put it in your beautiful carriage."

"Thank you, Raven," John responded. "I have been too much trouble for you," he added graciously.

"You are no trouble. You must come for many visits when the inn is complete, and I will give you more turbans and sashes. A fine brave like yourself needs to be able to choose each morning what to wear so that he might impress Indian maidens. Is not John a handsome young man, Dancing Leaf?"

I coughed and sputtered bean bread into my cupped hand. With such a thunder being as Raven, I reminded myself, one must always be alert. Normally she said embarrassing things to me alone, but now I was in the company of John Ridge. I could see that he was amused.

"It is true," I answered. "The other girls at the mission school often raced to prayer service, hoping to be the one who sat nearest to him."

John replied quickly enough without sputtering. "All except for Dancing Leaf. She preferred to sit next to my cousin Buck. She used to hide his slate from him, and once she spied on him when he was swimming nude in the river."

"It was the other way around," I protested, realizing too late how loud my voice was. I could see that John was enjoying this play, but still I did not want Raven to get new ideas about me. Nor did I want her to ask questions about Buck Watie, to whom I had given little thought after Blue Lake began attending the mission school.

I quickly excused myself to milk the cow, but when I arrived in the barn, I saw that Jonathan had already begun the task.

"Thought I'd help you get an early start," he explained. The bucket was already full, and he stood and lifted it. "The speckled pup is doing well. I'll watch him for you. He'll be ready when you come back."

I noticed then how tall Jonathan was. The top of my head barely reached his shoulders. His hair was the yellow color of the straw that lined the beds of the animals. The summer sun had blessed his skin with a warm, golden glow that contrasted well with his cream-colored shirt. Each morning his shirt was fresh and clean. The black book remained in his pocket, but he no longer removed it to read to me. Was he no longer a thunder being? And why was he not? I reminded myself that I must be alert.

"Will you return, Dancing Leaf?" Jonathan's abrupt question brought me back to the present world.

"And why wouldn't I?" I retorted, annoyance once again in my voice.

He put the pail down and stroked his beard as he looked at me. I realized that his beard was freshly trimmed. His hair was short and well managed also, and I wondered where his comb was. I had not seen it for some time.

"Well," he said, crossing his arms over his chest, "I know Raven's been bugging you to find a place of your own. And now that Blue Lake's gone . . . and this John Ridge will want a wife . . . and his family would probably like a new daughter."

"Ah, you are worse than Raven, imagining such things," I replied, but I spoke easily and not with the manners of a scolding wren. Still, I did not like that he had said *And now that Blue Lake's gone,* as if the future held no possibility of a return.

A breeze of sadness fluttered through me. "I will return for the speckled pup," I said quietly, but my voice broke, and my eyes suddenly brimmed with tears because of the many uncertain things. I was embarrassed and took several steps toward the door—I could not cry in front of this one the way that I did in front of Blue Lake.

I quickly exited the barn and took several deep breaths, but again a flood of emotion swept through me, for the world surrounding me was so beautiful. The orange sun, rising in the eastern sky, bathed the morning world in hues of gold. I looked to the outline of the hills on the horizon. The peaks were shrouded with ribbons of mist. I heard from afar the running water of the stream below. Grandfather Rock rested there, quietly overlooking Chera's grave.

Puffs of smoke escaped from the chimney of the cabin, and the scent of simmering squirrel meat lingered in the air. A fenced garden flanked one side of the cabin, and the newly constructed roof of the inn rose in the distance. I realized that one can love a place as one loves a person. My heart ached; I hoped I would not have to leave this place forever.

Jonathan was beside me then, and I took the full pail of milk from his grasp and began walking the stone pathway to the cabin. I did not hear his footsteps behind me, and when I turned, he remained standing there, watching me.

Ai-yee! Now I was the one with rude manners. I took several steps back to him and set the pail down. "Thank you, Jonathan, for all you have done," I said earnestly. "For killing the coyote and for taking care of the puppy and helping with the work of the inn. You have been a true friend."

He took my hand in his. "I'll say a prayer for your safe journey, Dancing Leaf."

If it had been the Jonathan of a few weeks past, I would have crossly told him that there was no need, that I had already said my prayers before the fire. But his words pressed softly on my heart, and I said simply, "Thank you."

He lifted the pail, and together we returned to the cabin, but he hurried to work on the inn and was not present to bid us farewell when our black carriage departed.

I knew the path of our journey because I used this same road when I traveled to the mission school at Spring Place. We would proceed south along the Great War Trace through Tennessee until we came to the Federal Turnpike near Red Clay. And then we would be in Georgia, where we would continue our travels until we reached Oothcaloga Creek, the creek of many beaver dams, where John's family lived. The mission school was not far from their home.

John and I sat inside the carriage, and Benjamin, the black slave, sat on the outside, guiding the horse. The morning was nearly half over before we left, and I doubted if we would make it by evening. The sun flooded through the window of the carriage. I shaded my eyes and remarked, "It seems the sun is angry with us this year. Her rays have scorched everything; there is no rest from her wrath."

"Dancing Leaf, Five Killer has told me of the sad loss of Chera. I am sorry to hear about this." His hand reached out and covered mine, and I was surprised by the gesture.

I tried to swallow the pain away. In the past few days I had forced my thoughts away from Chera so that I might attend to other matters.

"I remember when I first saw her as a puppy with Blue Lake," he added. "The two of them were always together."

The pain became a piercing one with this thought, and I wondered how the news would affect Blue Lake. Had he received my letter?

I turned to John, though, and posed the other question lingering in my mind: "Jonathan tells me the white man's Bible says that animals will not go to the next world. What do you think?"

I saw the flash of lightning in his eyes, and the words exploded from him. "Of course they will be there!" He paused and took a breath, and his next words were reassuring. "All of life moves on the same spiral. The Unakas may be smart about many things, but they do not understand the Creator's mind."

"That is true," I agreed.

"Nor do I," he said bitterly. "Sometimes I do not understand the Creator's mind. Death often seems a terrible tragedy." He reached into his pocket and retrieved a paper. "Here, I will read you the poem I wrote after Nancy's death." He unfolded the paper and carefully smoothed the creases. His voice was like a drum with a slow, steady beat.

On the Shortness of Human Life

Like as the damask Rose you see,
Or like the blossom on the tree,
Or like the morning to the day,
Or like the Sun, or like the Shade,
Or like the Gourd which Jonas had:
Even such is Man! Whose thread is spun,
Drawn out and cut, and so, 'tis done.
Withers the Rose, the blossom blasts,
The flower fades, the morning hastes,
The sun is set, shadows fly,
The sun is set, shadows fly,
The gourd consumes,—so mortals die.

"Ah, what a beautiful poem!" I exclaimed and reached my hand out that I might hold it. He gave the paper to me, and I read the poem slowly, giving the words time to rest in my heart. "Your writing reminds me of the verses of the writers who live across the waters in England," I observed, thinking that I should never show him my writing, which used only simple words. I did not even know what a damask rose was, nor a mortal. "Where have you learned to write so well?" I asked.

"I have read many of the white man's books. Next year I will travel east to a place called Cornwall, and there I will read even more until my education is complete."

"You're leaving your home? To travel all the way to the East?"

He nodded.

"Won't you be sad to be away from your family? Won't your mother be sad to see you go?"

"Yes," he replied with heaviness, and I knew then his leaving was no small matter. "Mother wants me to go," he added. "Both she and Father think I must learn as much as I can about the white world."

"So you can be a great Cherokee chief like your father?" I asked. "He is such a powerful and respected man."

John's eyes turned to the window and searched the distance as if answers resided in the outer world. When he looked again at me, I knew his thoughts had cleared. "Yes, he is a great man, but I am different . . . sometimes I am even angered by him. He often reveres the ways of the white world, while I think we should honor the old ways of our people."

I thought of Spider Woman and Talking River, who spoke similar words.

"And yet," he continued, "Father refuses to learn to speak the white man's language and sends me to learn these things."

We rode for a moment with only the creaking sound of the wagon wheels, and then we suddenly hit a rut in the road. We gripped our hands tightly to our seats but could not hold on. We both tumbled to the middle and became mixed up in each other's arms. Soon enough, though, we were righted and facing each other again.

"Yes, Father is an eagle," John resumed, "in both the Cherokee and the white world." His voice was light again, and I knew the dark thoughts had passed. "I would like to be so respected and admired, but I do not think I will be an eagle." He smiled. "And you, Dancing Leaf—will you follow the path of Nanyehi? She was perhaps the great-est beloved woman in the history of the Cherokee."

"I think there will be no more beloved women in the Cherokee world," I answered. "You have been to council meetings. Are there beloved women on the bench with the white chief and the red chief?"

John shook his head. "No," he answered quietly. He shrugged and added, "Many Cherokees today do not even know that such a rank once existed. I, myself, have never attended a meeting where a woman of this rank was present, and I'm not sure what her role was."

"A beloved woman," I explained, "was once equal in rank to a chief. She had the power of life and death over captive prisoners. She was called upon to speak in council meetings. Her word was heeded because the Great Spirit spoke to her in visions."

"Did she wear an eagle feather?"

"No, her emblem of distinction was a cape of swan's wings. When Beloved Mother made an important declaration, she did it with a wave of the wings, and no one was allowed to question her judgment."

"Do you have this cape?"

"Yes, I have kept all of her sacred things inside the deerskin box that she always kept near her sleeping mat. . . . When I think of these things, though, I'm not sure the swan wings or the title mattered so much. Beloved Mother had a way about her that I do not have. Everyone listened to her words. Everyone came to her for answers. It may never be that way with me." I noticed my tight fist had crumpled the material of my skirt as I talked. I smoothed the wrinkles and added, "Instead I have become a burden to those about me."

John laughed and poked a finger at my stomach. "You only think that because of Raven. I could see myself how she attempts to control you. Yes, she is strong and beautiful, but you cannot let her have your own power."

My eyes went to the window while John's words repeated themselves in my mind. Yes, Raven did try to control me. Why would I let her have that power? Why had no one said this to me before? Why had I not seen it myself?

"And besides," he added, "you clearly are not a burden to the others in the household. I have a feeling your opinion is more respected than Raven's."

That thought was a new one to me also. I had never heard anyone actually asking an opinion of Raven—not even Five Killer, who loved her.

"You speak with the wisdom of Grandfather Rock," I said appreciatively. "But still, I don't feel I have a place in this world."

"Nor do I," John assured me. "You worry too much, Dancing Leaf. I do not think of these things so often. What will be, will be."

"Yes, but you have a family," I argued. "You have a place to call home."

He stared at me, puzzled by my insistence. "You have a family also. Raven acts as if you don't because she is afraid of you."

"Afraid? How could she be afraid of me?"

"She fears that the land Long Fellow and Five Killer live on will one day belong to you and that in the future you will be making decisions about it. Anyone can see that she likes to be chief of the property—and how can she be if you are there? And once you start your own family, she thinks there will not be enough room for everyone, especially not her own daughter and children."

"Perhaps you are right," I reflected. "But Beloved Mother would have called Raven a thunder being, and she would have told me that I must learn to live with her."

"Yes, you must learn to live with her," John agreed, "but that does not mean you are to be controlled by her."

"But she is an elder," I reminded him. "I cannot question an elder or be disrespectful."

"And what would happen if you did?"

"I . . . I don't know. I have been taught not to, so I haven't, and I have thought no further."

"Well, I have often done both things." He smiled as he said this, and I laughed, remembering the arguments he had with the Gambolds. His father had even removed him from Spring Place because of the conflicts and had sent him instead to the stricter masters at Brainerd for a year.

"If I were in your place," John said, "I would see to it that Raven was the one who moved out of your home."

I laughed aloud at that thought. I pictured myself standing at the open door, pointing the way out to Raven, who dragged large bundles behind her, her head bowed. Of course, it would never happen. And besides, in a short time, the inn would be complete and she could move into her new home. Still, I enjoyed the image of her retreating form, and I laughed again and realized that I had not laughed for a long time.

"It is good to be with you, John Ridge." I reached over and took his hand.

"So now you prefer my presence to my cousin Buck's?" he teased.

"Yes, and now you will have to marry me," I teased back.

"I could do that," he persisted, still enjoying our game. "But what would we tell Blue Lake?"

"Ah . . . Blue Lake." Now the smile was gone from my face, and the lightness fled my heart. How quickly one's mood can change. "He has a family in Virginia. His white father. Perhaps he will stay there."

"I'm sorry. . . ." John searched for words. "It's just that I have always thought that one day . . . well . . . that one day you two would live as man and wife."

"What will be, will be," I answered, echoing his own words.

"Ah, yes," he said with a smile again upon his face. "Now you are adopting my own philosophy. I never bother to worry about whom I will marry."

We said no more for a length of time, and the wagon wheels continued to roll along the dusty road. As we entered a flat, treeless stretch, a brisk northern wind suddenly twirled the dirt on the trail. John took a cloth from under the seat and held it over the window to block the dust from rushing in.

"Do you remember the time you and Nancy spied on us boys— Buck, Blue Lake, Jeremy, and myself—when we were swimming nude in the river? I was so angry with the two of you for reporting us to the Gambolds. How long were you looking anyway? I always wondered about that." His eyes were dancing now.

I could not help but smile, too, thinking back to that time. "We looked for a long time," I admitted. "I was embarrassed, but Nancy was older, and she said that soon enough we would be married and that we needed to know about the differences between the body of a man and a woman."

For a moment I wondered what Mother Gambold would think if she heard me saying such things. When we asked questions of her, she would not answer, instead saying that these matters were to be discussed with us by our mothers and fathers. And Beloved Mother had told me when I was small that this matter of boys and girls was not treated in the same manner in the white world as in the Indian.

"We had similar thoughts," John said, "and one time we watched when you and Nancy were bathing in the river."

"When?" I asked, but already I knew the answer, for they were the ones we heard and not the ghost of Chief Vann.

"Of course, we did not tell the Gambolds and cause such a big ruckus because we enjoyed looking and did not want such things to come to a stop. Nancy was right. So why did you tell the Gambolds about us swimming nude?"

"Elizabeth insisted. She said you were doing an ungodly thing and that you must be stopped; she made us feel ashamed."

"I never liked Elizabeth." He rolled his eyes and shook his head. "Do you remember the time Buck lopped off a chunk of Mother Gambold's hair? He was trying to trim the bushes that grew along the walkway, and Mother Gambold bent over to show him what he was doing wrong. But he just kept trimming, and so he chopped off a large lock of her hair."

The image of the fallen hair came to my mind, and I saw also the expression on Mother Gambold's face when she noticed it. I burst out laughing, and John, too, laughed. I grabbed my knees to steady myself, I was laughing so hard, although at the time it happened, I did not dare to laugh.

"Remember," I asked as I went on with the story, "how her hair stuck up in front after that?"

"Yes," he answered, catching his breath because he, too, was still laughing. "Nancy used to help her pin it down each morning, but by prayer service, it was all sticking up."

We remembered other times then, too. Like the time the boys could not persuade the cow to come in, so we girls were sent, and we found her with a pretty brown-and-white-spotted calf. John remembered the time of the great storm when the roof was lifted and the boys sleeping upstairs found themselves staring at the moon and stars. The roof was found in one piece in the Millers' field two miles away.

I told him of the time Nancy's locket could not be found and then we saw Elizabeth wearing it, but Nancy felt sorry for her and told everyone she had given it to her. He told me of the time Nancy fell through the ice on the pond when they were small and how he ran with her in his arms for two miles until he reached a neighbor's cabin, where the two of them warmed themselves.

We were still talking when John's stomach suddenly emitted a low growl, reminding me of the growling baby bear. We stopped in a shaded, wooded area, and Benjamin took the horse to water while John and I removed our shoes, washed our feet, and splashed our face and arms. We brushed off our clothes because a fine layer of dust from the dry trail had settled upon us. The waterline of the creek was so low, the roots of the trees were visible and the ground was cracked like the shell of the turtle. Still, the water flowed steadily, and we were glad to have some.

When we had finished our meal, the face of the sun was no longer visible above the shimmering waves of the creek. So we built a small fire, rolled out our blankets, and slept under the boughs of a large oak tree.

In the morning, we returned to the carriage. This time, John and I sat on top of the bench with Benjamin so we could better take in the sights of the place that John called home.

The Ridges' plantation was not like the small scattered farms on the banks of the Ocoee; it was a vast homeland. We rode past orchards where peaches and apples grew and then through long fields of ripening corn. We came to a wide field with knee-high bushes.

"What crop is that?" I asked.

"Cotton," John answered. "It is the one crop that does well with the late summer heat. Have you never seen the cotton plant?"

"No," I admitted.

So John spoke to Benjamin, who stopped the carriage, and we stepped down to inspect the plant.

"Ah," John observed. "Already I see blossoms." He pointed to the flowerings of pink and purple. "After the flower, the boll will form," he explained, "and then finally this boll will burst, and the cotton itself will erupt from its center.

"We grow tobacco to the west of the house," he added as we climbed back on the carriage.

In the distance I could see the settlement of buildings that comprised the Ridges' estate. In the center was a large white house, and scattered in various directions were smaller buildings—a smokehouse, several barns for the animals, and storage buildings for corn, cotton, and other crops. Behind the large house were two rows of cabins for the slaves who tended the plantation.

We turned onto a shaded lane with poplar trees lining both sides, and the white house came into view again. The house had two rows of windows, one above the other. Inside I knew a set of stairs connected the two floors. A porch extended the entire length of the house. When we were closer, we saw John's parents and two other figures sitting on the porch, and also a gathering of people seated on the lawn.

"My family is still in mourning," John said, his tone somber now. "This is how it was when I left. Each morning my parents take their positions on the front veranda and receive visitors to comfort them. Today we will all proceed to the grave site for the proper service."

John stood and waved, and his mother and father both rose from their seats and waved back. I recognized one of the other figures sitting on the porch—Charles Hicks, a good friend and neighbor. He looked to be white but actually was a half-breed. The other man was a white man.

"It is Butrick," John said. "Do you know him? He is a missionary at the Brainerd school."

"I have heard of him."

Susanna, John's mother, was at the gate when we stepped off the carriage. "Ah, Dancing Leaf, how good of you to come," she said, putting one arm around her son and the other arm around me.

Major Ridge was more restrained, but he smiled broadly and took my hand in his in the custom of the white world. I said little while John answered his parents' questions about his journey.

We walked to the veranda, where the servants brought us plates and eating utensils, and we ate a meal of venison and roasted beef. The Cherokees in the yard were also fed. Among them were Ricky, the husband of Nancy, and the people of his family.

When everyone was full and the servants had cleared the yard, Major Ridge called out to the people gathered. "Let us proceed to the grave site, where Reverend Butrick will conduct the service for our beloved daughter, Nancy."

Together we walked a short distance to a small fenced yard with several stone markers. Nancy's grave, a mound of earth, was covered with flowers in the tradition of the white world. The people knelt, and I saw the look of surprise on Reverend Butrick's face, and so he knelt, too. Then he read from his black book, with John translating at his side. He read the story of the good shepherd, who cares tenderly for his sheep. He leads them to still waters so that they might drink, unafraid of the running stream. He has them rest in the soft green grass and keeps them on the true path.

When the reading from the story was complete, Reverend Butrick explained to the people that God is a loving Father who, like the good shepherd, will take care of us throughout our lifetime, even though it may be a short one, as Nancy's was. He explained that at one time there was no death and man lived in happiness in the Garden of Eden, but evil entered through the serpent. Only by the sacrifice of the Great One's own son, Jesus, are we able to live eternally with the Father again. If the people would accept Jesus as their Savior, he promised, we could all come to live together in the heavens above.

I liked this Reverend Butrick. He and Mr. Hicks dined with Major Ridge, Susanna, John, and me for the evening meal, which we ate at the large table many hours later. The sun had already gone down, and the Ridges' other children, Sarah and Watty, were in bed.

I could see that Major Ridge also had respect for this man, because he asked many questions about the God of the black book and his son, Jesus. Reverend Butrick did not speak Cherokee, so John translated; sometimes he tired and turned to me, and then I translated also.

Major Ridge seemed satisfied with the answers. On the last question, he leaned forward, and his voice was almost a whisper. "Reverend Butrick, I have killed men in my lifetime—many of them in the heat of war, which I know the Creator excuses. But once I killed a man in peacetime because he was a wicked Indian. Will God punish me for that? Perhaps I am punished with my daughter's death?"

Reverend Butrick's answer was swift, and his voice was firm. "No, our Father is a loving father. It is against the commandments to kill, but we must not live with evil men either. God knows that the purpose of your heart was pure."

"Well, I have resolved never to kill a man again unless ordered to do so in council."

"If you would convert, Major Ridge, then the Lord would always be in your heart to give you guidance."

Major Ridge shifted in his seat before he spoke again. "I cannot convert. The Gambolds at Spring Place have offered to teach me, but as I told them, I must respect the traditional ways of the Cherokee and honor the religion of my people. Still, I am glad that you white men are here to preach and to tell of good and evil, and I want my children to hear of the goodness of your god. Tomorrow we travel to Spring Place, where Susanna will receive instruction from the Gambolds. I believe that she will convert, and I will be happy for her."

Major Ridge stretched his hand toward Charles Hicks, turning the talk away from the white man's religion. "Charles," he informed us, "was head of the delegation that our council recently sent to speak with the white government. Twelve chiefs attended these negotiations. Charles will present the agreement made with the white president to the council meeting, which begins in a few days."

"We were received by Mr. Calhoun," Mr. Hicks began, "the agent of the President, a most respectable person. He is a good man."

Major Ridge nodded, and Mr. Hicks continued. "Of course, he talked again of going west. I explained that many of our people had relocated already, but those who remained were not willing to do so. They could not leave the land that had been given to them by the Great Spirit. They could not leave this tomb of earth where their ancestors rested. And the plants we use to cure our sick—our medicine men are afraid they do not grow in this western land. I reminded him the Cherokees who did move west were challenged by the Osage Indians, who laid claim to the same land."

I was relieved to hear that these things were being said, but I was distressed to think we were talking of these same matters again. Why must we repeat ourselves over and over to the white men? We did not want to move! Why did they always press us?

"Still," Mr. Hicks continued, "the white fathers insisted that we had more land than we could cultivate, and we were told that unless we were willing to share this land, our people could not remain here."

"Yes, that is what they always say," John remarked.

"We counseled with each other," Mr. Hicks went on, "and we were told by our white agents that we could be forced to move west. We were in agreement that none of us wished to be removed and that we were willing to sell some of our land, but we must be assured that no more demands would be made on the Cherokee who wished to remain in their homeland."

I looked to Major Ridge and then to John. We had given up more land? How could this be?

"What land was given up?" Major Ridge asked.

"Much of the mountain land in North Carolina."

I immediately thought of Talking River and Spider Woman. Was Coosa Town in North Carolina? Was that the reason Turtle Woman and her children had come to stay with us? Was that the reason Red Hawk traveled with a new delegation?

"The Black Mountain Range was ceded, but not the Smokies," Mr. Hicks added. "A large tract in Georgia and Alabama and an even larger tract in Tennessee were also given up."

"But at the last council meeting the chiefs agreed that no more land would be sold!" I could not restrain my outburst.

All eyes at the table turned to me, except for Mr. Hicks, who looked uneasily toward Major Ridge.

"Beloved Mother sent a message to that meeting," I asserted. "I myself put the words on the paper!" I remembered how desperately

Beloved Mother had wanted to attend the meeting, but Long Fellow persuaded her that the trip would be too difficult, and in the end she was satisfied that Five Killer delivered the message from the women's council.

"'Keep your hands off of paper talks!'" I repeated the words of that message now as I thought of them. "'The act of selling more land would be like destroying your mothers. Keep this land for our growing children, for it was the good will of our Creator to place us here. Listen to the talk of your sisters.'"

"She is right, Father," John said quietly. "We should not have to give them more land."

Mr. Hicks turned to me. "Yes, Dancing Leaf, you are right. But with the white world, it is always a matter of negotiation. We entered the meeting with fears that we would be forced—all of us—to travel west." He paused, giving his words time to settle.

"But," he continued, "we left satisfied that only these lands would be given up. Let me read to you the letter sent by the white government to our people." He reached inside his leather pouch and removed the paper and began reading it. "'I rejoice with you and thank the Great Spirit for his kindness to your nation. It was a day of darkness. You feared that you would be compelled to give up your houses, your cornfields, your rivers, plains, and mountains. The dark cloud has passed away. A good portion of your lands is secured to you; the wicked men who seek your hurt are to be kept from troubling you. You are allowed to sit quietly around your own fire and under your own trees, and all things are to be set before you and your children. Many have long been your friends, and now many more are coming to be your friends—hundred of thousands of good men and women in all parts of this country. Brother, it is the morning of a new and happy day.'"

Major Ridge pushed his chair back and said nothing, and I looked to John and knew his thoughts were the same as mine. To give away more land? How could it be a new and happy day? But the hour was late, and we knew that the discussions were over when Major Ridge stood, and so we all bid each other good-night. Susanna and Major

Ridge both accompanied me to my sleeping quarters, which had been Nancy's room in days before.

Susanna held up the lantern, and we peered into the room to see Nancy's younger sister, Sarah, already asleep on the large bed they had shared. "Dancing Leaf, thank you for coming to visit with us in this time of sadness," Susanna said. She reached forward and kissed my forehead.

"Before you retire," Major Ridge announced, "we would like to counsel with you about your future."

About my future? I looked at them in alarm. Had John told them of my problems with Raven? I was embarrassed to think that perhaps he had.

But Susanna spoke quickly to relieve my distress. "We have discussed it, the Major and I. We would be happy if you would stay with us. You would be like a daughter. John and Sarah and Watty would be happy to have you for a sister."

I searched their faces and saw that it was so, and I bent my head, and tears streamed down.

"Thank you, Mother. Thank you, Father," I answered softly, using the old custom of referring to caring figures in these terms. "Your words and thoughts are most kind. To live as your daughter would be a great honor, but I cannot at this time. I have had visions of my first mother, my birth mother. I believe that I must search for her. I will attend the council meeting in a few days, and I have hopes that I will find her or someone who knows of her."

Susanna put her arm around me again. "I can see how important this is to you, but you must know you are always welcome here."

And Major Ridge spoke also. "It is good that you attend the council meeting. I will ask the assembly myself if anyone knows of survivors of High Water. We will resolve this matter."

"Dancing Leaf must come to bed!" a voice called out from across the room, and we looked to see that Sarah was sitting up, demanding our attention.

Susanna and Major Ridge went to her bedside and bid her goodnight, and then we all said good-night, and Sarah and I watched as her parents retreated with the lantern down the hall. I saw in Sarah's eyes and cheeks echoes of her sister, Nancy. But Sarah was tall and thin like the major; Nancy had a smaller frame, like her mother.

"I cannot sleep," she confided to me. "Will you tell me a story?"

So I told her of the redbird who wanted to be an eagle.

"I will not be an eagle or a redbird," she said gravely after I finished the story. "I will be a beautiful swan, and many people will want to be my friend, and many men will want to be my husband."

"Yes," I agreed, smiling to myself and thinking that this one had the fire spirit of John and not the gentler nature of Nancy. "But you must remember that the true path of all Cherokee is to be a helper in this world."

"I will be a helper. I will do many things to help, but I will be a beautiful helper. And still I cannot sleep. Do you know more stories?"

I was not ready for sleep, either, and was glad to have a chance to remind myself of the many stories I knew. So I told her the stories that children love—of how the water spider captured fire for man and how the owl came to have a spotted coat and why the possum's tail is bare and how the bat and the flying squirrel acquired their wings.

She wanted me to tell her the frightening stories of Spear Finger and the raven-mockers, but instead, I said, "You should go to sleep with pleasant stories on your mind."

I was in the middle of the story of the race between the Crane and the Hummingbird when I saw that her eyes were closed. I paused for a moment, and she made no protest. Twice before, I had tried to stop, but then her eyes suddenly opened and she complained, "No, no, tell me more. I was not asleep. I was only resting my eyes."

She had not had an easy day, I judged, for with the service, she had been forced to say good-bye to her sister. I blew out the candle and went to sleep myself, but soon enough I was awake because, once again, the child of my dream world appeared.

I looked to the window and turned my thoughts to the Great One above. "Please reveal the meaning of my dream," I implored. "If there be any survivors of my family, I pray that we be reunited." I paused to let my thoughts travel to the upper regions. "Help me find my path in life," I added. "I want to be a true helper."

My thoughts went to Nancy, and for a moment I could feel her presence in the room, along with the babe who had died with her. I sang in my heart the song of the seven heavens, and I sang it seven times, that the two of them might rest in Galunlati with the many ancestors who had traveled there before.

STAR WOMAN

Asga Ya Galunlati, the father of all, had a daughter whose beauty was as bright as a star. One day while she was in her father's garden, she heard a drumming noise. She was curious, so she dug a hole to see where the drumming was coming from. When she bent to look in, she fell into the hole and went spiraling down from the seventh heaven toward the earth below. Creatures lived upon the earth then—creatures of feeling but of no mind—they were waiting for the spark of mind to come to them.

The father could not call his daughter back, so he sent strong winds to support her and inspiring thoughts to the earth creatures that they might help her. This was the time when the earth was covered in water, and the creatures floated upon it.

Turtle was the first to offer help. "She may land upon my back; we must make it strong."

Water Spider dove deep down and brought up a bit of earth and placed it on Turtle's back. The bit of earth grew and grew. Great Buzzard flew above it, flapping and dipping his wings to create mountains, hills, and beautiful valleys where people might live.

Star Woman spiraled down for many days until finally she came to rest upon the earth. From her came life as we know it today. Her breasts gave corn, beans, and squash; her tears formed rivers of fresh water. Her blessings lighted the spark of mind. All human beings can trace their roots to Star Woman. One mother is the mother of us all.

Chapter 9

Major Ridge, Susanna, and I left at sunrise the next morning to travel to Spring Place. Susanna was to receive her weekly instruction, and I was anxious to visit with Mother and Father Gambold, whom I had not seen since the death of Beloved Mother. They would be surprised to see me. I hoped they would not chide me for not returning earlier to visit.

When we reached the grove of trees that rimmed the pool of spring water, we paused to stretch our legs and let the horse drink his fill. Sometimes the water murmured as it gently swirled from under the white ledge. At other times it was perfectly quiet and still. The spring was a special color—green, but unlike the green of grass or trees or any of the other works of the Creator. We children thought it a magic pool, and we often made up stories, saying a town of Cherokee people lived below. When the townsmen moved about, the water rippled, and when they slept, it was still.

We dipped our hands into the pool and soothed our throats as the encircling trees sheltered and cooled us. Then we mounted the coach and rode past the orchards of cherry, peach, and apple trees that Father Gambold tended.

The settlement came into view, and I saw that nothing had changed. The blockhouse buildings were placed in a square with open space where we students could enjoy the sun and breeze. In one corner was Mother Gambold's herb garden with many medicinal plants. Some of these plants I did not know, as they came from the land across the great water; some she grew because I had showed her the plants we

Cherokee used in our medicine world. Susanna often sent for medicines when her children were sick.

The horse's hooves clopped softly on the dry, red dust, and the creak of the wagon wheels echoed from the empty buildings of the school settlement. I squinted and peered through the late morning haze, but the only motion was the flutter of the curtains from open windows. The children had all returned to their homes for summer stays, and it seemed that we had traveled to a ghost place. The spell was soon enough broken when Father and Mother Gambold appeared on the front porch, waving their arms as the Unakas do and crying out warm words of welcome.

"Dancing Leaf, what a wonderful surprise!" Mother Gambold embraced me before the others, and I was touched by her warm gesture. "I hope you are returning to stay. We need a teacher for the little ones."

"I would like to, but I can only visit at this time."

I stepped aside so Major Ridge and Susanna could extend their greetings. Mother and Father Gambold had not changed, I reflected as I observed them. Mother Gambold's gray hairs were tightly knotted at the back of her head. Her black dress was faded and crumpled in the folds, but her starched, white apron rested stiffly across the front of her dress. Father Gambold's wisps of white hair sprung about in different directions on top of his head, but it grew more densely in back and curled where it touched his collar. He removed the curved pipe from his lips to greet us and grasped our hands each in turn.

"Father, show Major Ridge how well your cherry trees have done despite this drought," Mother Gambold instructed her husband. "And cut some bear's bed fern for Susanna; she likes to use it for John's bad hip.

"And Dancing Leaf," she said before I had a chance to wonder what task I would be assigned, "how fortunate that you have come. We have a new charge—a very young girl. Come see. She's in the schoolroom." Mother Gambold threaded one arm through mine and the other through Susanna's, and the three of us strode together to the closed door of the classroom. "I think she is perhaps five or six years old," she continued in a soft voice. "Her name is Maggie."

Then Mother Gambold made a face and leaned in closer. "Dancing Leaf, I can do nothing with her! She refuses to learn her letters and spends her lesson time drawing pictures on her slate. She is a most unhappy child. She never smiles."

Slowly I opened the door, and we peered inside the quiet room and saw the small girl with long, black hair sitting at a desk near the front of the room.

"She is supposed to be copying her alphabet letters," Mother Gambold said in her whisper voice. "I told her she could not have a midday meal until they were all copied." She patted my arm as if to say she knew I could handle this charge, and then she and Susanna slipped away for their lesson.

I watched the girl from behind for a few moments. I thought she had surely heard us whispering in the doorway, but she did not turn to see who was there. She continued with her head bent forward, her fingers busily making marks on the slate. I took steps forward, and when I was close enough, I could see the figures she had drawn—stick people—perhaps a mother, a child, and a small creature at their feet.

"Who are these people you draw so well?" I asked as I peered over her shoulder.

She did not look at me but continued working, as if it were a common occurrence to have a perfect stranger watch from behind and talk about your work.

"I see a woman and her child," I ventured. "And perhaps this is their dog."

"It is not a dog," she said without looking up. "It is a turtle."

"Ah, yes," I agreed. "I see he is close to the ground and he has no ears, but a tail and four legs."

She turned abruptly and asked, "What is your name?" She had a round, moon face, with large, half-moon eyes of black. A sparkle of crystal light emitted from the center of each one, reminding me of a bright star on a dark night.

"My name is Dancing Leaf."

"What is your other name?" she demanded.

"I have no other name."

"You do not have an English name?"

"No," I said softly. True, many Cherokee had both a Cherokee name and a white man's name, but no one had ever pressed me to take one, and I realized at this moment that I had never desired one either. "And what is your name?"

"The Gambolds call me Maggie, but my Cherokee name is Star Girl. My mother called me Star."

I agreed with Mother Gambold's estimation—the child looked to be five or six years old. She was probably the same age I was when I was an orphan child and came to live with Beloved Mother. I thought for a moment of how I must have looked to those about me at that time. I smiled at her and said, "Star is a beautiful name."

She did not smile, but her dark eyes continued their piercing stare as if they were on the mission of a vision quest. I knew that more questions would be asked, and I would not be the one asking.

"You will call me Star," she announced in a confident voice. "I do not like to be called Maggie. Why are you here?"

"I have come with the Ridges to visit. I once went to school in this place as you do now."

"Where are your parents?"

"I do not know," I answered. "I was at one time an orphan child. My adoptive mother died . . . last fall." I stumbled through the words as the thought came to me that yes, nearly a full year had passed. The drowning pain of that time was not so overpowering now, but still I did not wish to revisit it fully, and I forced my thoughts back to the child who sat before me.

"The Gambolds say I am an orphan, too, but this is not true. My father brought me here because he lost my mother. He could not find her." She held up a small finger as she talked, in the same way Mother Gambold often raised her finger for important words, and I thought that yes, the child was learning some things at this school.

"I will find her," she continued, her finger stabbing the air, "but someone must help me look." She paused to measure the effect of her talk on me. And then she leaned closer and said in her child voice, "Every night in my dreams I call to her."

"Yes," I answered slowly, and then I was the one who paused, giving myself time to connect the vision before me with the vision of my dreams. "Yes . . . you must find her . . . I have heard you in my own sleep calling for your mother."

It did not seem possible—the child in my dream world, a child of real flesh and blood, sitting before me now in this schoolhouse? But my words did not surprise Star, for she said, "Yes, you will help me find her," as if the decision had been made long ago. But her next words were a question—"How will you help me find her?" And I knew my answer would have to meet her approval.

"Tomorrow," I responded with resolve, "I travel to the council meeting. Major Ridge has promised to make an announcement that I am looking for my mother. He will ask if anyone knows of other survivors from High Water, the town where I once lived near the Creek villages. I will tell him about you, and he will make this announcement for you also."

She tilted her head, and her eyes lifted skyward as she considered this matter.

"Many Cherokee people will be present," I assured her. "Surely someone will know of your mother."

Her dark eyes rested on mine, and then she crossed her arms, and her next words were a pronouncement. "I will go with you to this council meeting. My mother may be there. She will know me when she sees me. Is it far?"

"It is not far. But we must ask Father and Mother Gambold's permission, for they are your caretakers." I picked up the slate. "Why are you not making your letters as Mother Gambold has asked? I am told we can have no midday meal until these letters are finished."

"I am not hungry, and I do not like to do what the old ones say."

"Your mother would not like to hear these words," I scolded softly. "She would teach you that we must always respect the gray hairs, for they are our teachers, even when we don't like what they say or do." I watched as the words traveled to her heart.

She nodded lightly. "Yes, she would say that. I will do letters, and you will do some also, and we will be finished soon."

"No, you will do all of them. I can be a helper and show you how, but you must do all of them."

She took the cloth and wiped away the stick figures and, with no further words, busied herself making letters. She wrote quickly—all twenty-six letters. Then she placed her slate on the desk and directed me to plait her hair in the way mine was done so that she could feel the breeze on her neck.

"You will tell them that I am going with you," she said as my fingers worked through her silky, black hair.

"No, we must ask. We do not tell our elders what is to be done."

Mother Gambold was surprised to hear our happy chatter and to see this peaceful child with plaited hair, her alphabet laid down before us. She was so delighted that she insisted that Father Gambold and the Ridges come and admire Star's work. They praised her fine, straight letters, but the girl shrugged their words off as if it were only a small accomplishment.

She has no manners! my silent voice cried out as I lifted my thoughts to Beloved Mother in Galunlati above. Much time had passed since I had sent such thoughts to her. I would need her counsel in the days ahead, I judged, for this star child was an unusual child, and I did not have the experience of a mother to counsel me.

I did not rebuke Star, though, in the presence of the others, because the voice of Spider Woman traveled to me: *Young hearts are connected closely to the spirit world from which they came, and we must take care to honor the spirit in each child.* So my next words were light ones. "Star, let us sing for Major Ridge. He always enjoys the voices of children singing." Major Ridge's carriage never left until he had heard the children of the school gathered in song.

"Yes, come," Mother Gambold agreed. "It is time for our noon meal, and you two will sing the blessing song."

When the others were seated at the long table, Star and I remained standing, our hands joined. I began singing softly, but soon our voices rose together:

> Bless this food, O Lord above
> Fill our hearts with peace and love
> For all good things we know you bring

Heavenly praises we will sing.
Bless our friends, O Lord, we pray
Keep them safe both night and day
No evil thoughts lead us astray
Send your love to light the way.

Major Ridge was so well pleased that he clapped his hands, then reached down and lifted Star in his arms. We were all surprised at his action. Susanna often embraced children, but I had never seen her husband do so. Perhaps Star reminded him of his own Nancy when she was a small child. Star surprised us also, for she did not turn aside or struggle to be put down, but smiled and placed her head on his shoulder while he held her.

Mother Gambold's face brimmed with a large smile, but I saw that her hand rested on her heart, and I saw also the pain in her eyes. I had seen this pain before.

"You must lie down and rest after our meal," I insisted, and I rose and placed a chunk of rabbit stew on her plate. I took the bowl of potatoes and carrots also as it was passed down, and filled her plate so she would not have to do so. She made no protest, and I knew this pain was a serious matter.

"The doctor ordered her to rest each afternoon," Father Gambold informed us, "but she lets many afternoons pass without doing so."

"But you must!" I pressed. "Today you will lie down—and every day after this. Do you have heartleaf in the garden?" I asked.

She slowly turned her head from side to side, and Father Gambold spoke for her. "There's a few dried leaves in the cabinet. I'll brew them when she's eaten. But, Dancing Leaf, could you scout about for more? We're nearly out; there's none in the garden."

"Yes, I will do that." I ate quickly and excused myself before the coffee was served. "Come, Star, you will go with me."

I knew that heartleaf loves to grow in damp places, protected from the rays of the sun. I had found it before near the stream in the wooded area behind the field. I grabbed the small basket from the hook on the kitchen wall, then I took Star by the hand. Together we headed for the stream.

"Do you know how to take a plant from its home to use as medicine?" I asked as we journeyed across the field.

She shook her head and listened gravely as I explained the procedure of passing over the first, second, and third plant and offering a petition to the fourth. At the edge of the running waters, we removed our shoes and waded southward until we found small clumps of heartleaf growing beside a fallen limb. Together we counted, pulling up every fourth plant, until we had a small bundle that we carefully placed in the basket. I unfastened the pouch around my waist and shook out several kernels of corn. I handed them one by one to Star, who placed them on the ground where the plant had been.

"Thank you, oh beautiful heartleaf," I said in proper petition. "Your medicine will be well used. It will make Mother Gambold's heart strong and free again. We leave these kernels of corn to show our gratitude."

Star carried the full basket as we walked hand in hand across the meadow brimming with life. Tall flowers with brown eyes and yellow feathers swayed gently in rhythm with the wind. Insects chirped noisily, and black birds with red-tipped wings dove around us. The dry grass tickled our ankles as we walked. The haze of the morning had cleared, and the sky was a dome of blue. A feeling of peace and joy burst forth in my heart and slowly infused my body. I took Star's other hand, and together we danced in small circles across the meadow. We were breathless when we reached the other side, our faces red with heat and our hair moist with perspiration, but our spirits were light with joy. I would have liked to have rested there at the edge of the meadow, bathing in the sunlight and good feelings, but the thought of Mother Gambold, clutching at her heart, urged us back.

Still, we skipped along merrily, until we crossed the boundary of trees that encircled the settlement. There the enchantment was broken. I stopped abruptly and drew my breath sharply, for a dappled horse was tied to the hitching post.

"That's my horse, Red Sky," I said to Star. "And that is our wagon, too." I pointed to where it rested under the shade of the oak tree.

The Gambolds and the Ridges were seated on the front porch, and a tall figure stood in front of them. When the standing figure turned,

I recognized Jonathan Young. Not bothering with the steps, he jumped off the porch and walked with hurried strides to meet us.

His smile of greeting faded when he saw the fear in my face, and he spoke quickly, "Now don't get into a pucker, Dancing Leaf." He nodded a greeting to Star. "Five Killer's the one who sent me to find you."

"What is wrong?"

"Nothing's wrong. Why don't you introduce me to your friend first?" he asked easily.

For a moment, I met his question with a flash of anger, for I was embarrassed and annoyed to be reminded of good manners by a thunder being—and one who often lacked good manners himself.

"My name is Star," Star said before I had a chance to speak. "What is yours?"

"I'm Jonathan." He reached his hand out, but Star pulled back until I took her hand and put it into his.

"Are you Dancing Leaf's brother?" she asked.

"No," Jonathan and I replied in one breath.

"Will you be her husband?" she asked next.

"No!" I answered. Ai-yee! How was it that this one had learned no manners? When the two of us were alone, I would explain that we must not ask such questions.

Susanna called out, "Come inside with us, Maggie. We are going to have some cake before we begin the journey home. Dancing Leaf needs to speak with Jonathan."

Star skipped forward, but she looked back several times, and I wondered what questions were forming in her mind. Susanna gathered the rest of them, too, to go inside, for they would have preferred to sit and listen to our talk.

When the door was shut, Jonathan and I went forward onto the porch. He stretched his hand toward me, but I held my arm stiffly and kept the distance between us.

"I am frightened to see you here," I informed him. My eyes searched his for a sign of bad news . . . perhaps Long Fellow. . . .

"I didn't mean to scare you, Dancing Leaf." He reached for my hand again, and this time I did not pull away. "Let's sit down."

We seated ourselves on the porch, and I nervously smoothed my skirt. I could see that he, too, was uneasy, because he removed his white hat and pressed his fingers along the edge, turning it in a circle several times before he finally spoke.

"It's nothing bad," he said. "Five Killer and Long Fellow sent me here. They want you to come back as soon as possible because of problems with the inn. The agent from the government office in town came by with a paper. I don't know what the paper says, but I'm told we have to stop working on the inn until I bring you home."

A paper? He had come to fetch me because of a paper? "What words could be on this paper?" I asked.

"I don't know, but Long Fellow says you're the only one who can straighten out the matter." Jonathan lightly tossed his hat up and then caught it with two hands before he placed it on his head again.

"Why did you not read the paper and talk to the agent?" I asked.

"I tried to, but Raven said it was Cherokee business and I was to attend to my own things . . . and, well, you know Raven. She wouldn't let me look at the paper, even though neither she nor Turtle Woman can read."

I could think of no papers that would hold up the work of building an inn. "But the council meeting begins the day after tomorrow," I informed him. "Five Killer knows I must attend. I cannot return at this time."

"Well. . . ," he began, but then no words came to him, and he rose and crossed the porch and rested his hand on the pole that supported the roof. His eyes searched the trees in the distance and did not look at my own as he continued. "Five Killer mentioned that. He said I should go with you to this council meeting and bring you back quickly when your business was finished."

I did not like to be so pressed. I saw the faces of the others and wondered who felt such urgency. Surely not Five Killer, who rarely hurried. No doubt, Raven was the one who pressed for action, and no doubt she had decided that Jonathan would accomplish this mission. I said nothing as these thoughts presented themselves to me.

Jonathan broke the silence. "Dancing Leaf, Raven said that perhaps

John Ridge would want to bring you home himself, and if it was so, I could return on my own." He turned his face, and his eyes studied mine.

My heart was stirred because this thought of John seemed to trouble him. "No," I answered softly. "John Ridge has much to do at this council meeting. His father is the head chief."

Jonathan rested his back against the pole of the porch, and his next words were swift and light. "Well, then, I will be the one to travel with you. I don't mind a bit, Dancing Leaf. Besides, I like the idea of meeting the Cherokee chiefs."

I did not tell him that perhaps I minded that we should be traveling and staying together in the week ahead. Had no one thought it improper—an unmarried young man and maiden staying together? Raven had given it thought, no doubt, but the plan had probably been her design. If I was not to be with John Ridge, then surely my time with Jonathan would prove fruitful to her wishes. But it angered me only a little, for with the thoughts of Star and the possibility of finding my birth mother, I could not mind so much these games the others played. I wondered, though, what Jonathan's true feelings were. Was he glad to be with me or simply glad to have a chance to bargain with Cherokee chiefs about the building of his church?

"But it may be several days—even a week," I told him. "I do not know how long this business will take."

"That long?" He lifted his hat to the sky. "What's so important about attending this meeting?"

So then he was annoyed, and I, too, was annoyed with him once again.

"I search for my family," I said evenly. "My first family," I explained when I saw the questioning look on his face. "I was an orphan child before I came to live with Beloved Mother."

"Yes, I know," he answered, and I wondered how he knew, because I had never told him. "You could come home first and then go back," he suggested, taking a step toward me.

"No!" I exclaimed, stomping my foot on the wooden step. "This matter cannot wait. And Star, too, is an orphan and wants to look for her parents. Why did not they send this paper with you if it so important?"

"I don't know." Jonathan's hat stayed on his head, but he lifted his arms straight to the sky. "I don't even know where it is." He shook his head. "Raven seemed afraid that I would find it and read it or that one of the others would give it to me. I think she may have hid it even from them."

I sighed. "Well, this problem with building the inn will have to wait a few more days."

Star was in the doorway then. "Susanna says you are to have some cake now," she announced.

I rose and took her hand. "You must call her Mother Ridge," I counseled.

Jonathan followed behind us.

"Susanna is one of my best pupils," Mother Gambold boasted to Jonathan as our forks sank into the rich, yellow cake set before us on Mother Gambold's fine china plates. "Next spring she will be baptized—on Easter—when we celebrate our Risen Savior."

Jonathan pulled himself up straight, his face beaming in the way that the rising sun beams warming rays. "Blessed is the man who walks not in the counsel of the ungodly," he quoted from the Bible to Susanna, "but his delight is in the law of the Lord."

The Gambolds were impressed to hear this scripture, and soon Jonathan was explaining his studies and his desire to lead a congregation of believers in our settlement. He continued to quote Bible passages as he talked. I did not like that he was showing off, but the Gambolds thought otherwise and offered verses from their own memories.

"I am pleased that you bring light to these people," Mother Gambold encouraged, "for some of them are so savage. We have pupils who strip down to their loincloths to play ball. I am told that those who live in the mountain villages hold wild dances around fires and chant and sing in heathen voices. It frightens me that we cannot reach all of them."

My thoughts went to Talking River and Spider Woman and the others in the mountain village, and I thought to issue a protest, but then

I looked to Major Ridge, who did not understand English. Besides, he was glad enough to have his people instructed in the Christian way, and Susanna made no protest either. Nor did I wish to trouble Mother Gambold's ailing heart. I worried that her excitement in talking with Jonathan was even too much.

As the Ridges readied to leave, everyone agreed that Jonathan and I would stay behind until the next day. The Gambolds were eager to spend more time with a young white minister, and Jonathan was thankful to have time to discuss the matter of Christian instruction to Cherokee students. I was glad for extra time to inquire about Star's past and also to ask that she be allowed to travel with us. I waited until time to retire for the evening before asking, however.

"She wants to go with you?" Mother Gambold seemed to think it a most unusual request. She looked to Father Gambold in confusion.

"Well, Dancing Leaf," he answered thoughtfully, "we had hoped you would remain with us while the child was in our care. But I see that your mind is decided. You seem determined to attend the council meeting."

"Anna," he said, addressing his wife, "we cannot keep Star here— you have said so yourself—and she has found a kindred spirit in Dancing Leaf. Perhaps they will return when the council meeting has ended," he added, looking to me with a question on his face.

"I do not know," I answered truthfully. "Star and I both search for our families of origin. What do you know of her parents?"

"Very little," Mother Gambold answered. "She was put upon us by Billy Wildhorse, who claimed that the child was his brother's. The child's father, he said, had traveled to Arkansas to live with the Cherokees who had crossed the Mississippi River. The child's mother, we were told, worked and lived with an old white man and woman, which is why Star speaks English so well. Billy Wildhorse said Star's mother died after a violent fever, but Star wouldn't believe this or be comforted by the old couple, and so they asked him to bring her to our school."

"We don't know for certain," Father Gambold said. "Billy Wildhorse recited the story as fast as he could, and then he was gone."

"These things have happened before," Mother Gambold added.

"Perhaps Billy Wildhorse was the father and there is no brother. Anyway, he didn't want to be bothered with the child."

"How long has she been here?" I asked.

"Only since the early winter," Mother Gambold answered, "but she says that she lived with Billy Wildhorse for some time before she came here."

I wondered why Star believed her mother still lived, for surely she must have died, because there had been no one to claim Star. But had I not had the same thoughts about my own mother?

Jonathan was sent to sleep in the boys' quarters, which were the rooms above the schoolhouse, and Star and I retired to the extra bedroom next to the Gambolds' room. But we tossed and turned, unable to sleep, and a thin slice of moon beckoned to us from the window. So we slipped our moccasins on and rolled up our blankets to carry with us, and we quietly made our way to the running waters of the creek.

Small stacks of firewood were neatly piled by an ashen pit that the children used for afternoon picnics on spring and fall days. I carried flint rocks in my pouch, and after much chipping and fanning, the small sticks of tinder finally produced a small flame.

"The smoke will carry our prayers to the Creator above," I explained to Star.

"I do not know how to say a prayer," she objected.

"You only have to say what is in your heart. I will go first." I took a pinch of tobacco from my pouch and sprinkled it in offering to the fire. "Thank you, O Great One," I said, "for bringing me safely on our journey. Thank you for Father and Mother Gambold. Thank you for this one, Star. Tomorrow we travel to the council meeting to search for our mothers and our families. Guide us in our search. Help us find our families. We give thanks."

I turned to Star and handed her a pinch of tobacco. "Now it is your turn."

"But you have said it all," she replied quietly.

I looked at her with stern eyes and would not look away until she sighed and scattered the tobacco in the fire.

"Thank you, O Great One, for Dancing Leaf. I know she will help me find my family." The words were scarcely said when she turned to me and asked, "Can I see the rock you carry in your pouch?"

I was surprised at her request. How had she known about the crystal? I had never spoken of it. But this child seemed to know many things without being told, and maybe she had felt it when we sat closely together. I retrieved it from my pouch and placed it in her open hand. "The crystal is a special crystal given to me by a friend. Often I hold it in my hand when I pray."

Star held her hand toward the firelight and tilted the crystal in various directions, observing the light on the different faces of the stone. Finally satisfied, she held it to me and said, "I see a star in there."

"You do?" I asked. I had often searched the crystal myself, hoping to find a special message, but I never had. I looked to the place where the tip of her finger rested.

"It is the morning star," she informed me, "rising over a clear, blue lake."

THE BOOK

The Creator made both the white man and the red man. The red man is, however, the elder brother, and so the Creator gave him a book.

Now, the red man was instructed to study the book and thereby improve his life. But he was not interested, and he carelessly left the book lying around.

So the white man stole it, and now the book is the property of the white man.

The Creator has said that it should be so, and the red man is to make his living with the bow and arrow. It is not for the red man to have the writing.

Chapter 10

We ate a breakfast of peaches and cherries and eggs and bread. Jonathan excused himself to tend Red Sky and the wagon, and Father Gambold followed. Mother Gambold seemed in no hurry to have us depart, and she sipped coffee while Star and I washed dishes and returned breakfast items to their proper shelves. I was glad to see that Mother Gambold's lips were pink and not blue. Surely the heartleaf had worked its medicine.

"You must come back after the council meeting, Dancing Leaf," she encouraged. "See how Maggie is taken with you?"

"Yes," I agreed, but I glanced nervously at Star. I did not like that Mother Gambold talked about her as if she weren't there.

"I have trouble with the full bloods," she continued with a sigh. "We're getting five new ones in the fall. It's difficult at first with the younger ones who like to take off their clothes. They don't want to learn to read and write, and they spend too much time gazing out the window. You come and teach them, Dancing Leaf, and they will be more willing. You can speak to them in Cherokee."

"It would be good to be here," I answered, dusting crumbs of bread to the edge of the table. "But I can make no plans until I find my family," I reminded her.

"What about this young man . . . Jonathan?" Mother Gambold asked, setting her cup down to give the matter full attention. "I think he has eyes for you, Dancing Leaf. He is a good man."

It seemed strange to hear him called a "man," although I myself did not think of him as "the Unaka boy" any longer. I brushed the crumbs into my apron, and when I looked up, my eyes were caught by Mother Gambold's.

"You would do well to cultivate his friendship, Dancing Leaf," she urged easily.

But I knew she suggested something more than friendship. I opened the door and shook crumbs into the wind, and when I stepped back in, Jonathan and Father Gambold were standing in the opposite doorway, so I made no reply to her. In the crook of Jonathan's arm was a stack of books.

Father Gambold rested his palms on Jonathan's shoulders and declared, "You will find this reading most beneficial."

My hand went quickly to my mouth, pushing back the cry of surprise. Books are greatly treasured in the Unaka world. How could Father Gambold have been so easily persuaded to part with them?

"I'll return your books next trip back," Jonathan assured.

"You must take good care of them," I said sharply.

The Gambolds looked at me with startled faces, so I turned my back and arranged the dishes on the cupboard shelves. But I reminded myself that these two did not know Jonathan as I did. He was quick to take advantage, and although he had proved himself a willing helper, I did not trust his motives.

Jonathan wrapped the books in his bedroll, and then the three of us—Jonathan, Star, and I—placed our blankets under the bench seat of the wagon and climbed in. Jonathan sat in the middle, with the reins looped through his fingers. The Gambolds stood at the front of the schoolhouse and waved farewell. Their arms swayed from side to side, reminding me of a dog's wagging tail.

"Have you been to this place before—New Town?" Jonathan asked me after we rounded the bend and the school was no longer in sight.

"No, but it is not far from the Ridges' plantation. Father Gambold said we were to follow the Consauga River to the point where it flows into the Coosawatie, then we will be there. We should arrive well before nightfall."

The morning air was cool, and clouds of vapor nested in the meadowland that bordered the road. I tugged at my shawl, pulling it close.

In the western sky, a thin ribbon of moon lingered, but I knew it would soon fade from view. My eyes scanned the tops of trees, and I noticed the yellow leaves scattered about. The previous evening Star and I had lain by the fire and listened as chanting cicadas announced the coming of shorter days. Soon it would be time to bring in new corn, and the children would return to the schoolhouse.

A sadness pressed upon my spirit, and suddenly the matter of finding my mother did not seem so urgent. I longed to return home, to the cabin of Long Fellow. Surely there would be a letter from Blue Lake; another full moon had passed, and we were nearly at the time of the dark moon now. My eyes went to Star, though, whose bright eyes danced with the possibility of reuniting with her mother.

Jonathan's thoughts must have been similar to mine, for he turned to Star and asked, "What is your mother's name?"

A moment of silence followed, so that both Jonathan and I turned to see if she had heard the question. Suddenly the name tumbled from her mouth. "Rebecca," she said softly. "Rebecca," she repeated in a louder tone of assurance. "I was very small when I lost her." She then turned to me. "What is your mother's name?"

"I don't know," I answered swiftly, for I knew it would not help to think long on the question. Many times I had struggled to find the memory, but it hid from me. I could not remember her name or her face, nor could I remember my brother.

"When I see my mother again," Star announced confidently, "I will know her. She wears a blue calico dress with ruffles, and she twists her long hair into a bundle above her neck like Susanna does."

Jonathan and I exchanged smiles, for we were amused by Star's gestures. Her small hands drew invisible circles at the bottom of her skirt to demonstrate the ruffles, and then they went to the back of her head, and she twisted her fingers to show us how this bundle was made. I could hardly believe she was the same child who had sat stiffly in the school the day before with her slate of stick figures.

"I don't know if she will know me," Star continued, "for I have grown . . . this much." She held her hands apart the length of a forearm. "But when I tell her, 'Yes, I am Star Girl,' and when I show her the place where the raccoon bit me"—she lifted her skirt and showed us the half-moon scar—"then she will be happy to see me again."

"Say, I've been bitten by a coon myself." Jonathan loosened one hand from the reins, pulled back his sleeve, and twisted his arm so Star could inspect his own scar.

The two of them went on to talk of other encounters with woodland animals, while my mind dwelt on matters at home. I wondered who was tending our garden, since Raven did not like to work in the hot sun. I hoped Turtle would see that it was cared for. I thought about my writing, for I had neglected it the past few weeks. I longed for the time when I could record more stories.

When my thoughts drifted to Chera, I took deep breaths. If only I had left her sleeping with her puppies in the barn, or if only I had taken the gun with me, then I would still have Chera and the red pup that so resembled her.

My fingers went to my waist pouch, and I fingered the crystal rock inside. Blue Lake's face dawned brightly in my mind—such a clear picture that it startled me—his dark hair and his round, blue eyes. A feeling of intense yearning gripped my being. I was glad when my thoughts were drawn back to the present world by Jonathan's question to Star.

"Do you know Jesus?" he asked.

"Does he have short black hair that sticks up on top, and does he grunt when he turns pages as he reads?" she asked thoughtfully.

I laughed aloud. "No, Star, that is Benjamin Crowsfoot." Benjamin was always a source of amusement at the mission school. "Jesus is a person who lived a long time ago, long before the mission school was built. He does not walk about in the Cherokee land at this time."

"Then how could I know him?" she asked Jonathan.

I kept my face forward, but I let my eyes slide sideways to observe Jonathan. I could see that he was not so amused, and I did not wish to annoy him. Besides, I was interested to see how he would answer this question. If he intended to persuade Cherokee children to accept Jesus, then he must tell a very fine story indeed.

He wasted no time and began with the story of a traveling mother and father who stopped at a barn for the birth of their baby. He told about the sky full of angels, who sang for joy, and three wise men, who traveled from a far country, bringing rich gifts. Star listened intently, but she frowned when Jonathan spoke of death on a cross, and then her questions poured forth so quickly that Jonathan could not keep up with them.

"What is a cross?" she wanted to know. "Was there blood everywhere? What is a tomb? How did he escape from this tomb? How old was he when all of this happened? Did he have any children? What about his mother? Why did she let the bad men take him?"

Jonathan responded to all of her questions, but Star was only more confused, and her questions continued to pour forth. He and I were both relieved when we heard the sound of wagon wheels and horses' hooves and distant voices.

"That's the Federal Turnpike Road up around the corner," Jonathan remarked.

Where the two roads converged, Jonathan reined Red Sky to a stop, and we waited while a large wagon with a father, mother, grandmother, and three children passed in front of us.

"Are you headed to the council meeting?" Jonathan called out.

The people in the wagon only looked at us, although the father nodded.

"They do not understand English," I informed Jonathan. I did not volunteer to call out in Cherokee, though, for it is not our custom to intrude loudly with rude questions. Besides, I was sure they were going to the council meeting. And when I shaded my eyes and peered farther down the road, I saw more wagons—some with high hoops and canvas covers.

As the afternoon progressed, more travelers joined us on the road. Those on horseback swiftly passed us. Sometimes small children and mothers rode on drag nets behind the horses. Star studied the faces of the passing women, and I knew she was searching for her mother.

The sun had just passed the midpoint of the sky when we came to the place where the rivers flowed together. When our wagon moved out from under the canopy of trees and into open space, we were presented with such an array of sights and sounds that we all three stood up at once and held our breath while we strained to take it all in. Cherokee people of all sizes and ages were engaged in many tasks.

The voices were merry, and the figures were all clothed in the brightest of colors—blue, red, yellow, gold. Handsome braves with turquoise turbans wore engraved silver bracelets. Some wore beaded necklaces. Their leather boots were fringed with strips of leather.

Young women were clothed in blue calico skirts, red sashes, and white cotton blouses. Their black hair shone like raven feathers. Many of them wore it plaited down their backs. Several wore large coils on each side of the head. I had never seen this style before, but I thought it most becoming. Still others pulled their hair back into soft bundles on their necks.

The savory scent of roasting meat soon drifted toward us, and I noticed rows of smoky pits along the eastern edge. Birds and pigs rested on spits, as did the hindquarters of deer and cows. A large wagon off to one side was filled with stacked boxes of squawking chickens. Along the western edge, women bent over stone ovens, removing loaves of white bread and small mounds of corn bread. Scattered about were blankets in bold colors, topped with baskets, pottery, clothes, jewelry, and even iron pots. I thought of Raven when I saw a blanket with bright scarves, turbans, and skirts. In the very center of the activity, I observed two large pavilions held erect by poles lashed together. The next day they would be filled with people for the opening ceremonies.

Jonathan pointed to the procession of wagons that continued along the river. He urged Red Sky forward, and we joined the others, so that we, too, could make a camp close to water. The wagons pulled into resting spots in succession, and I was glad to see that trees shaded the spot where our wagon turned. Jonathan took Red Sky to water and then tied her to the tree so she could graze. As we watched her pull on the tufts of grass, we realized we were also hungry. We made our way to tables of food, where we were given hunks of meat, ears of roasted corn, and chunks of bread. We wandered about while we ate, observing the handiwork of weavers, basket makers, silversmiths, and other artisans.

Star, however, was not swayed from her mission, and her eyes intently searched the faces of women we passed. I hoped she did not appear rude, but I did not worry, for I was so taken by the lively gathering.

We retired to our campsite when finally our bellies and eyes were full and could take in no more. Jonathan and I stretched a canvas between two trees and placed our wagon beneath it. Then we rolled out our blankets onto the soft grass, and neither of us wanted to lift ourselves up again until we had rested. But Star, still bounding with energy, announced she would gather firewood so we could have an evening fire.

"You must go no farther than the pine tree on the east side or the white wagon to the west," I warned. "I do not want to lose you."

She looked carefully in both directions and promised, "I will go no farther."

Although I intended to keep my eyes open for Star, they soon were closed, and when I opened them only a short time later and looked in all directions, I did not see her. I called out to her but heard no answer. I pivoted four times and called out from each direction, and still I heard no reply. My heart leapt with each breath, and I tugged on Jonathan's arm till he rose to help.

"There's still plenty of light left," he assured me. "And she can't be far. These are all good people. Nothing bad could happen to her."

We set about in opposite directions, calling her name. We made small circles outward the first time, but then we traveled in larger circles, three times returning to check with each other.

Jonathan remained calm. "She's safe, Dancing Leaf. It's just a matter of finding her."

A cluster of children had gathered at the campsite next to ours, and I approached to ask them to help with our search. But when I was close enough, I saw Star sitting with this very group. Her face was bent to some engaging task that had all of the children entranced. Laughing and talking as they worked, they were so caught up that they heard nothing else.

"Star," I said loudly, but I had to repeat it once again before her eyes lifted.

"Dancing Leaf!" she exclaimed, and then her hand clapped over her mouth. "Oh, Dancing Leaf, I forgot about gathering the firewood. But see," she said, pointing to the tree at the boundary, "I went no farther than I was allowed."

I looked at her curiously. In one hand she held a piece of charred wood, and her face and hands were smudged with black. On the ground before her was a slice of newly cut wood with black letters. The other children also had these charred pieces and cuts of wood. I knelt down to see the marks they made, and although the figures resembled the letters of the alphabet, they were different in other ways. I could not judge what words they were writing.

"What are you doing?" I asked politely, for the children seemed kind enough.

"I am teaching them how to write in Cherokee," said the girl in the center. I judged her to be a few years older than Star. "I am Ahyoka. My father is over there. He is the one wearing a turban." She pointed to a man who was himself the center of a gathering of five Cherokee men talking with grunts and gestures, their faces glowing with the liveliness of their talk.

One of the small girls at my feet was not to be interrupted by my intrusion, and she tugged on Ahyoka's sleeve and demanded, "Show me again how to write *Redbird*. It is my mother's name."

Ahyoka made three letters resembling a *V*, a *J* with a closed loop, and a *G* with a tail.

"Look, Dancing Leaf, here is my name," Star said, holding up her slate of wood with three letters that were similar to *Z, P,* and *B*.

"But this is not the writing we learn in school," I insisted, for I did not wish these children to be fooled by this play activity.

"It is not white man's writing," Ahyoka said. "It is Cherokee writing. My father invented it." She tilted her head in the direction of the men.

I looked to her father again, wondering why he would invent such a game for these children—it would only make it more difficult for them to learn the real alphabet. As I studied him, I was impressed with the fine quality of his style. His clothes were a blend of the Cherokee world and the white world. A blue turban with red roses and white posies was wound about his head. Around his neck was a scarf of red cloth. From his right ear dangled a large gold earring. He wore a blue tunic bordered in black. A silver-handled knife hung from the beaded belt around his waist. His pants were plain buckskin, and when I looked more closely, I saw that one side was not filled out the way the other pant leg was. He leaned upon a cane.

I turned my attention back to the matter of the markings on wood. "The letters resemble alphabet letters, but they do not make the same sounds. How is it these marks make the word *Star*?"

"Each mark makes a sound," Ahyoka explained. She pointed to each mark and said the sound, and then she pronounced each of them in succession, and yes, the word was *Star,* which has three syllables in Cherokee. "At first Father drew many pictures, and he decided each picture would represent a Cherokee word. But there were too many pictures and too many words, and even he could not remember all of them. So then he made a picture for every sound instead of every word. You must learn eighty-six marks for eighty-six sounds, and then you will be able to write in Cherokee!"

Can this be true? I wondered. *Cherokee words from a Cherokee alphabet of sounds?* "How many words can you write in Cherokee?" I asked.

"All of them," Ahyoka replied. "You say a word, and I will write it."

"Blue jay," I ventured.

She drew three letters—*C,* an *H* with a tail, and a capital *S* with a line through it.

"Spoon," I tried next.

Ahyoka made three letters—the middle one looked like a *V,* and the first and third resembled an upside-down *V.*

Star picked up the task then, rattling off a series of words—*squirrel, hill, corn, bread*—and for all of these, Ahyoka wrote Cherokee words.

"How long does it take to learn this writing?" I asked.

"Yellow Bird," she said, pointing to one of the children, "learned it all in three days."

"Three days?" I was surprised, for Yellow Bird could not be more than eight years old.

"She has taught it to her mother also," Ahyoka added.

Still I was skeptical and wondered if these children were not simply "playing school" and if Ahyoka perhaps knew no alphabet at all but had made up one for her own amusement. I remembered the days before I went to school. I would sit with a slate for hours, making letters that I pretended to be true writing. Perhaps these children were just playing.

My thoughts were interrupted by a group of older boys who approached us with jeering faces. Two of them stepped forward, crossed their arms, and peered down at the writing.

One of them carried a long, ivory-handled knife in his belt. He spit on the ground and called out to Ahyoka, "Your father is a man-witch. He practices black magic with his strange marks. You must all be his witch children." He pointed accusingly at the children's writing, and then he looked back to the other boys, who murmured their agreement.

The children stopped writing and looked at Ahyoka. She did not look at the boys but continued to make marks on wood.

"He uses those marks to cast spells on people," declared the boy with the long scar curving down his cheek.

The children's faces filled with alarm, for many of them had been taught to fear the spells of witches, especially the raven-mockers, who steal the hearts of dying children.

"It is not true," Ahyoka countered as she lifted her gaze to meet the eyes of the small ones gathered around her; she continued to ignore the ill-mannered boys.

The boys moved in closer, and the one who carried the silver knife announced in a loud voice, "Yes, it is true. My uncle lived in Willstown, where your father once lived, and he told me that they ran your father out of that town. They burned down his cabin. They scared him so badly, he has never been back."

"Where is your mother?" the scar-faced boy taunted. "She will no longer travel with your witch-father, will she?"

The small girls rose from their knees and backed away from the circle. I put my arm around Star, and the two of us took several steps back, although I did not believe that Ahyoka's father was a witch. I spun in a full circle, searching for Jonathan, but he was not in sight.

"There is no bad magic here."

I turned to see who spoke with such assurance.

The man Ahyoka had pointed to as her father spoke again. "I do not look like a witch, now do I?" In one hand he held a pipe with a very long stem. He paused to breathe in the tobacco, and he blew the smoke in the direction of the boys. "I am Sequoyah," he announced. "Yes, perhaps the writing is magic, but it is good magic, and I will show you how it works."

He smiled and gestured to the boys to come closer. They strode forward like strutting roosters, their heads held high and cocked to the side as if they dared this man to try his witchcraft on them.

Sequoyah stooped down and picked up a piece of the charred wood. "Perhaps your mother is not home," he began. "You want to tell her you have gone fishing, but how can you, if she is not there? Well, see, you simply make these marks." He drew a series of marks on the dried wood. "Now when your mother comes home, she reads the words you have written for her—*I have gone fishing*—and she is satisfied to know your whereabouts."

The boys said nothing, but they continued to look at the dried wood as if the marks were cursed.

"Come with me," he said to the one with the scar. "We will see if this magic works."

They walked some distance, until we could no longer hear what they were saying. The boy whispered in Sequoyah's ear. Sequoyah picked up a piece of charred wood and wrote on a slab of bark. Then he strode back to Ahyoka and showed her the marks he had made on the bark.

"Screech owl," Ahyoka said.

The boy nodded his assent, but still he did not appear assured, so they performed the same procedure with five more words—*wolf, rain, apple, go, see*. Ahyoka recognized each word immediately upon seeing the written marks. The boys did not seem pleased, however; perhaps they believed the myth that said only the white man should have a book. But the small children were delighted and soon were on their knees again, busily making their marks on the shaved bark of the tree, until only the father and I were left standing.

"I am Dancing Leaf," I said quietly, "daughter of Nanyehi, beloved woman of the wolf clan from the peace town of Chota."

"I am Sequoyah," he answered. "I see that you have already met my daughter Ahyoka."

"So, what Ahyoka says is true?" I asked. "With this alphabet we can write words in Cherokee, perhaps even send letters back and forth to each other?"

He smiled and nodded. "Yes, many times I have done so." He paused to draw from his pipe, then added, "Of course, it was a project that required only twelve years of my life. And what the boys said was true—my neighbors were sure I was practicing witchcraft by working long hours in my cabin and making strange marks on paper. And my wife was convinced also, so that I was forced to leave when she burned down my shed. With the fire went my first five years of work, and I had to reconstruct it all from memory. But I was determined."

His words were not angry words, though, and I told him how much I admired his patience.

"Perhaps I am possessed by a little madness," he confessed. "It has not been easy for my family. Ahyoka has been a true gift from the Creator. She is drawn to the Cherokee writing, as I am, and insists on going everywhere I go. Her mother, of course, would prefer that Ahyoka remain at home with her and the other children."

"Can you write in the English language also?" I asked.

"No," he scoffed, "and I have never learned to speak it either, nor do I intend to. But I think the talking leaves have helped the white people make many advances. And now we Cherokee will make similar advances with our own writing, and we soon will have no need of them. We will once again live as a proud and independent people."

"You don't believe the myth that says only the white man should have a book?" I myself did not know what to make of the myth, and I often hid my writing when elders visited.

"Of course, truth resides in every myth! We know that the white man stole the book from the red man, and since the Creator originally intended it for us, our duty is to get it back. That's what I believe, and creating a Cherokee alphabet has been my method of accomplishing this task."

"I want to learn how to write in Cherokee. I have already begun to record the stories told to us by grandfathers and grandmothers for many generations, and it would please me greatly to record these stories in the Cherokee language."

"Learning is easy enough," he said. "Ahyoka is only nine, and she is my best teacher."

Sequoyah and I now stood alone in twilight, as the children had returned to their camps. All along the river, people gathered in small groups by their fires, and the air was full of happy voices and laughter. Jonathan called to me to join him and Star.

"You are welcome to sit with us, too," I invited.

Sequoyah declined my invitation, saying he wished to retire, but when he discovered that Ahyoka was already at our campfire, he sat down, too, and asked questions about Beloved Mother and Five Killer, whom he said he had fought beside in the Battle of Horseshoe Bend.

We talked for several hours. The little ones fell asleep, and we wrapped their blankets around them. Sequoyah told me of his work with silver and offered to show me the jewelry and spurs and other pieces he had made. He talked also of his travels to Arkansas on the other side of the big river.

The words he chose were eloquent, and I was surprised he had not taken the trouble to learn the white man's language. I judged him to be a mixed blood, for his skin was light and his face long and thin. He had been raised by his mother's family, and he did not speak of his father, so perhaps he was angry with the white side of his family, and perhaps that is why he had little to do with their world.

Jonathan, of course, did not understand our Cherokee talk, and he had fallen asleep soon enough after the small ones. When he began to snore loudly, sounding like a snorting horse, Sequoyah picked up Ahyoka and bid me good night.

So then I was alone with Jonathan and Star. She was fast asleep and had not so much as twitched her nose for several hours, so quietly she slept. But Jonathan's snores grew louder and longer, and I became distressed when I heard the rustle of bodies in neighboring camps and saw heads pop up to look our way. When someone threw a rock at Jonathan's feet, I knew I must do something. I kneeled beside him and rolled him onto his side, and the snoring immediately stopped. I breathed a sigh of relief and was soon myself in the land of dreams.

We rose at daybreak. Jonathan walked Red Sky to limber her legs, while Star and I retrieved bread from the women who baked. When we finished our breakfast, we walked with the others toward the pavilion. Ahyoka remained with us on the eastern side of the pavilion, while her father, a warrior of distinction during the Creek wars, sat in the area near the front reserved for those of special rank.

Jonathan declined to sit with us. "I wouldn't feel right," he said. "The seats are for your people." He planted himself along the western edge and was soon joined by other white men. Two of them looked to be traders, for they were dressed in the buckskin clothes of traveling white men, but the other two were surely ministers, for they wore dark shirts and pants and small black hats.

The benches quickly filled with people. When I turned and saw row upon row of faces, I was reminded of the meadow behind the mission school, where flowers of many colors sway in the summer breeze. The brightly colored clothes, the gold and silver jewelry, the turbans, scarves, and sashes—I had not expected such richness. My mind traveled back to a council meeting I had attended with Beloved Mother when I was a small child. The people then wore simple clothes of brown deerskin. Beloved Mother had sat with the chiefs and other head men, her cape of swan wings resting on her shoulders.

The bench reserved for the head men of the nation was empty for the moment. Who would be sitting upon it on this day? Not a woman, I reflected, for John Ridge believed that the rank of beloved woman no longer existed.

My question was soon enough answered, for through the vista of trees, a troop of horsemen appeared, riding two by two. Major Ridge, mounted upon his beautiful chestnut horse, led the procession. The crowd, which had been talking in low murmurs before, now sat in total silence without even the whimper of a small child.

The chiefs dismounted, and attendants led the horses away. The chiefs then stepped forward in formation, approaching the seats of honor reserved for them.

White soldiers, I reflected, all wore clothes of the same color and cut, but no two of our chiefs were dressed alike. My eyes were drawn to Chief Lowry in his cream-colored tunic with two braided sashes that crossed in front. A pendant of gold, the size of a child's fist, rested on his chest. His gold loop earrings were so heavy, they weighted his earlobes and pulled them into long pendulums. A small gold piece dangled from his nose. The other chiefs were in simpler styles, but they all wore beads, silver pieces, feathers of distinction, and scarves of bright colors.

Major Ridge was dressed in a dark coat and pants in the style of the white man, but a scarlet ribbon was tucked inside his vest. The leather band around his head was decorated with the eagle feather of the head chief. He was a mountain of a man, and when he began the opening speech, his words poured forth with the rhythm and force of an approaching band of horses. His voice carried so well that the criers in the center did not need to repeat his statements for those in the back.

He welcomed his people and congratulated them on the progress made since the last council meeting. Our children attended schools, our women made their own cloth with spinning wheels and looms, and our men tilled the soil. The Cherokee land was resplendent with stately houses, barns and fences, and fields of fine crops and well-tended gardens. The white world could easily see what a strong and self-sufficient people the Cherokee had become.

When he paused, murmurs of approval rippled through the audience. He waited for quiet, and his next words were intoned softly: "We must do all that we can so no more land will be taken from us."

I felt a rush of relief.

"And we must resist all attempts to entice us to move from the land of our fathers to the unknown territories on the other side of the Mississippi!" His voice had grown louder with each word, and the murmurs from the crowd were now a soft roar.

When everyone quieted, he continued. "Our task at this council meeting is to pass laws so that we can be a self-ruling nation. We have no need for the limits set upon us by the white world."

All around me I saw smiling faces and nodding heads, and I felt the spirits and hearts of the people soaring. Just a few days earlier at Major Ridge's home there had been talk of selling more land and moving west, and my mind had been uneasy. But I knew that he had been conferring with other chiefs since his arrival here, and as he spoke now

I heard the resolve in his voice and felt the strength of agreement from those around me. If only the white world could be persuaded.

My eyes scouted the edges of the gathering. I was pleased to see several soldiers in uniform standing toward the rear, and I noticed also two soldiers busily writing on paper, sitting at the table with our own scribes. These men would surely report this talk to the white fathers in Washington, who would be persuaded of our resolve and leave us to peace on the land that was rightfully our own.

Chief Ridge removed his handkerchief, wiped his brow, and took the seat of honor reserved for the highest chief. Two drummers then entered the pavilion from the rear and beat soft rhythms as they swayed up and down the aisle. A troop of dancers, painted with the red-and-white stripes of victory, followed. They circled east to west, then west to east, as they stepped toe-heel, toe-heel. The turtle rattles attached to their legs echoed the beat of the drum.

Chief Going Snake made the second speech; he thanked the many people for traveling from distant places. He resumed his seat, and Major Ridge produced a twist of tobacco and passed it among the chiefs. Each one cut off a small piece for himself.

Father Steiner, a white man, was asked to preach. He told the crowd about the love of the Father God for all the peoples of the world. He asked for God's blessing upon this council, and he prayed that all of the Cherokee people might come to know their Lord and Savior, Jesus Christ. He spoke in English words, pausing for Chief Hicks to translate to Cherokee.

Lame Deer, the adawehi, was called upon next. He began by invoking the spirits of the four directions, pivoting north, south, east, and west, his palms pressed together in reverence. He drew from his pipe and fanned the smoke upon the seated chiefs. He murmured as he did so, but his words were ancient, sacred words that none but the priesthood understood. He took another puff from his pipe and blew the smoke out upon us. Finally his eyes rose to the spirit world above, and he called upon departed elders and chiefs in Galunlati to look down upon us and to be pleased with our work and to protect us from any bad doings. When he finished, he handed his pipe to the chiefs, who passed it among themselves, and he seated himself on the ground near the bench.

Major Ridge came forward again and called for one of the scribes to read the order of business for the day. I listened carefully to the matters for review, but when I did not hear mention of a call for lost relatives, a feeling of unease clawed at my stomach. I fingered the crystal in my pouch. There were so many important affairs to be decided; my request seemed small and insignificant in comparison, and maybe Major Ridge thought likewise, or perhaps he simply had forgotten. And yet it was no small matter for me. Besides, I had promised Star that we would have this opportunity.

She tugged on my arm after the scribe finished reading. "When will they ask about our mothers?"

"Soon," I whispered, "but we must not talk when the chiefs are talking. Be patient."

Fortunately both she and Ahyoka had brought slabs of wood, and they busied themselves practicing Cherokee letters. I saw young John Ridge sitting at the table of scribes, and I vowed to speak with him about this matter of lost relatives when the time was right.

Many laws were passed during the next few days. I wanted to report them all to our neighbors and friends, so I carefully recorded with my own pen and paper each law as it was adopted. The nation would be divided into eight districts, and each district would have a court, judge, and marshal. The marshals would collect a poll tax of fifty cents from every family and deposit the money into the Cherokee National Treasury. All children were to attend school. The practice of having more than one wife would no longer be tolerated, nor could a white man living with a Cherokee wife have both a white wife and an Indian wife. White men would not be allowed to work as clerks in the nation unless they were given special permits. White families would not be allowed to rent land from Cherokees, and any Cherokee who broke this law would have to pay a sum of five hundred dollars and would receive one hundred stripes from the whip on his bare back.

For three days I recorded the laws declared in the council meeting. In the evenings I practiced the Cherokee writing while Star and Ahyoka played with other children. Jonathan, in the meantime, was delighted to make the acquaintance of so many Christian Cherokee. We saw little of him, but I often observed him in the distance, talking and reading from books with Cherokee Christian ministers like John Arch and David Brown.

On the evening of the third day, I approached the table of scribes, where John Ridge was himself busy with pen and paper. "John," I began timidly.

"Dancing Leaf!" he exclaimed, and he was not at all timid. He came around the table and put his arms around me. "I'm glad you came to talk with me. Many times I've looked up to see you sitting out there. Are you enjoying the council meeting?"

"Yes, but I have come to find my mother." My words tumbled out hurriedly.

He looked at me, puzzled for the moment, and said, "So you didn't come to talk with me? You have more urgent matters?"

"Yes, I am happy to see you!" I smiled at his teasing. "It's just that your father said I might address the council to ask if anyone knows of my family."

He looked to his father, who was busy in discussion. "I will speak with him," he assured me. "I will see that your concern is the first item addressed tomorrow."

The next morning, Star and I arrived long before any others, and we chose the bench closest to the front. As the procession of chiefs entered, I held my breath. When Major Ridge rose, my heart sank for a moment, for I felt that I was no more visible than a field mouse. I could not bring myself to wave my hand or call out as the Unakas do. Star also sat quietly. To my relief, however, Chief Ridge's speech went straight to the subject of missing relatives.

"Many Cherokee families have been wrenched apart," he began, "by the wars we suffered in years past with the white world. Some still search for wives, husbands, children, mothers, and fathers. We are gathered here today from all parts of our nation—from the mountains of the East to the forests of Alabama; some have even come from the land west the Mississippi. If there be any among you searching for missing relatives, I ask that you present yourselves now. Dancing Leaf, who was adopted by our own departed beloved woman, Nanyehi of Chota, will come forward first."

I rose and made my way with trembling knees to where Chief Ridge stood. "My village was called High Water, and it was near the Creek land." My voice sounded thin and weak and warbled like the call of the gray marsh bird. I waited as a crier in the center repeated the words for those in the back.

"High Water was destroyed by Unaka soldiers nearly ten years ago," I continued, my voice growing more steady and strong. "I know that I had a small brother and a mother, but that is all I know. I am searching for other survivors of my village. I hope that my own family escaped to the mountains."

Once again my words were echoed by the crier, but the moments that followed were moments of silence. The others looked about to see if anyone would respond. When no one did, they cast their eyes upon the ground, perhaps in respect to my pain. I sighed and looked to Chief Ridge, because I did not know what was to be done next.

He stepped forward again. "We will appoint a special scribe to record these facts," he said, nodding to the table of writing men. "Those of you gathered today may pass the word along to others who are not present, and if anyone knows of survivors of High Water, they will tell the scribe and he will write it down. Dancing Leaf can check from day to day to see if anyone has come forward."

Embarrassed, I only wanted to return to my seat quickly, when a small figure suddenly beside me proclaimed in a loud voice, "I am Star Girl. I am six years old. My mother is Rebecca. She has been lost for a long time. I did not want to go with my father across the big river because I know my mother is here." She pointed to the ground. "I know she is not there," she added, pointing to the outside world across the Mississippi.

Amused faces nodded to each other. Chief Lowry stepped forward and lifted Star to his shoulders. "Some of you," he said as he turned in a slow half circle, "may have not been able to see this Star Girl."

There were many smiles then, but no one came forth to claim Star either, so she also was sent to the table of scribes. A line formed quickly, and the matter of lost relatives became the business of the entire morning, with many people coming forward to announce their search for family. In that time only two people were reunited—a grandmother and her granddaughter, who was a mother now herself. We were all touched to see their happiness, for tears of joy sprang from their eyes as they embraced.

For the next three days, Star and I checked with the scribe, and still no one came forward with information about our families. The crowd of people dwindled as families returned to their farms for harvest. The major issues had been decided, with the remaining details to be worked out by council members.

On our last day, Sequoyah and Ahyoka demonstrated Cherokee writing. The chiefs and people were impressed, and I heard no talk of witchcraft. The council declared that the scribes would learn this writing. All business would be recorded in Cherokee and English, and a newspaper for the nation would be printed in both languages.

As we unrolled our sleeping mats and pulled our blankets over us that evening, warm thoughts of home flowed through me, and I realized how eager I was to return. But I worried about Star. Would she expect me to continue searching for her mother? Perhaps Billy Wildhorse's story was true and her mother had died of a fever. I wondered if I should tell Star what had been told to me.

Star lay on our blanket, gazing at the stars. "My mother has gone to the Sky World," she said softly.

"Your mother has gone to the Sky World?" I repeated as I turned toward her. I could hardly believe she was saying so and wondered who had informed her. "How do you know this?"

"Jesus told me," she answered.

"Jesus? When did you talk with him?"

"Last night."

"Did you see him?"

"No, but Jonathan said you can ask Jesus anything, and he will always answer you. So last night I called out to him in my mind, and I asked him if he knew where my mother was."

I sat up and looked at her. "What were his words?"

"He said, 'Star, your mother has crossed the pathway of the stars, and she lives in the sky kingdom above. She loves you and watches you and promises to wait for you there so that you can be together again someday.'"

"That was a lot—what he said to you," I answered softly and lay back down.

Star then sat up. "You should ask him about your mother, Dancing Leaf."

"I don't have to," I replied, for in my heart I knew the answer. "My mother, too, has gone to the Sky World."

WHY TURTLE'S SHELL IS SCARRED

Turtle and Possum, who were very good friends, found a plum tree. Possum could climb easily now that his tail was bare, so he ascended the tree and threw the tasty plums down to Turtle. They laughed and talked as they worked—that is, until Wolf came along.

Wolf was very hungry and jumped in the way, catching the plums intended for Turtle. Possum waited for the perfect opportunity and then fired one straight into Wolf's mouth, where it lodged in his throat and choked him to death. Turtle cut off Wolf's ears and used them as spoons when he ate his hominy.

Of course, the wolves heard of this and were greatly angered. They took Turtle prisoner and held council. Their first thought was to put him in a clay pot and boil him, but Turtle only laughed, adding he could easily kick such a pot to pieces.

Next they decided to put him in the fire. Again he laughed and declared that it would take no effort to put the flames out. So they decided to drown him in the deepest hole in the river.

Turtle trembled at this and pleaded, "Oh, no, please, anything but that."

Happily they dragged him to the river and threw him in—which was, of course, just what Turtle wanted—and he swam safely under the water to the other side. However, Turtle had landed on a large rock when he hit the water, cracking his back into twelve pieces. Immediately he began singing a medicine song:

I have sewn myself together,
I have sewn myself together,
I have sewn myself together,
I have sewn myself together.

The song was powerful, and soon the shell on his back was whole again, although you can still see the thick seams of the mended scars.

Chapter 11

"Where will be our home?" Star asked the following morning as we prepared to leave.

All around us, families gathered belongings and packed wagons. Jonathan hitched Red Sky while I doused the fire.

"Star, I cannot say at this moment." I handed her the edge of her blanket while I held the other side, and we stepped forward and brought the ends together. "You need a new blanket," I advised. This one had been patched in many places, and even the patches were now thin. "Put it under the seat."

I watched as she did so, her question traveling through my mind again: *Where will be our home?* She had said *our* as if we would remain with each other without question.

We were only a few miles down the road when she spoke again. "I don't want to stay at school with the old ones unless you stay, too."

Neither do I was the thought in my mind, but I answered, "We will have to wait and see."

I had lain awake the past evening for several hours, tracing the possible routes our lives could take. The first step, I knew, would be to return Star to the Gambolds. I could not assume responsibility for her, since she had been left in their care. Besides, I was not old enough to act as a mother. I had no husband to act as a father, and despite John Ridge's assurances, I was not sure I had a place I could call home.

The next step would be to return to Long Fellow's cabin to see to this matter of the paper that was holding up the building of the inn. Perhaps the Gambolds would allow Star to travel with me, but they would likely insist that she return, and they would press me to return with her also. Living with the Gambolds and teaching at the mission school would not be a bad life, I mused. Father and Mother Gambold were kind and cared about us in the way parents do, and Star and I could be together.

But perhaps news had arrived from Blue Lake. Maybe he had returned. And if he had? Too many questions remained. I could not know these things until I arrived home, so I simply squeezed Star's hand and told her not to worry. She made a sour face and kept her head pointed forward for several miles. When we arrived at the Spring Place mission school, she lifted her skirt over her eyes and refused to put it down.

The mission school was once again a ghost place, and it did not come to life as it had the week before. Jonathan reined Red Sky to a stop, and we sat attentively, but we heard no voices. The windows were drawn shut. I did not smell the smoke of the morning fire or the usual aroma of pig's meat that Mother Gambold cooked for breakfast. Jonathan and Star remained in the wagon while I climbed the steps to the front door. I knocked loudly and called out, but no one answered. The white knob on the door would not turn.

"Maybe they went visiting," Jonathan ventured.

"They do not visit," I told him. "Everyone comes here. Besides, they were expecting us to return."

Star and I sat on the steps while Jonathan tried the back door.

"Someone is coming," Star said.

I listened and heard the horse's hooves pounding the lane. A black horse emerged from under the trees first, and when the figure came into view, immediately I recognized Jeremiah Ashbury, who lived with his family near Spring Place. He had no brothers and sisters, and his mother often sent his outgrown clothes for the children of the school. He rode his horse fast and hard and did not rein him in until he was nearly at our feet. We stood, and Star took several steps back, tugging on my hand.

"I have bad news," Jeremiah said, not waiting to dismount. "Mrs. Gambold passed on four nights ago."

"Mother Gambold?" I stepped backward myself, as if forced by a sudden blow. Yes, I knew she was sick, but she had been sick a long while, and she rested and took her medicine, and always her voice was strong. I thought she was stronger than death and wondered how she could depart so quickly. "She has died? I cannot believe it!"

Jeremiah nodded.

"Was it her heart?" I asked, clutching at my own.

"Yes. Doctor Butler was on his way to see what could be done. She died before he got here."

"Did not the heartleaf help?"

"Ma said she didn't think anything could have helped. She died peacefully, Dancing Leaf. In her sleep."

"Where is Father Gambold?"

"He left yesterday for Brainerd."

I had never been to Brainerd, but I knew of it. John Ridge had attended a mission school there for a year.

"Maybe he'll stay on with them for a while," Jeremiah added. "I don't think he can keep the school going without Mrs. Gambold."

Nor did I.

"He asked if you would take Maggie with you, Dancing Leaf. He says he can't be a proper caretaker for her. Mrs. Gambold would want you to find a proper home for Maggie—that's what he said."

I breathed a long, deep breath, and Star entwined her fingers in mine. "Yes, yes," I agreed. "Star will come with us. I will see that she is well cared for."

We gathered flowers from the meadow—yellow ones with dark eyes, white ones with yellow eyes—and placed them on the mound of earth Jonathan found behind the schoolyard. He read a passage from his black book before we resumed our journey.

Always before, when a loved one died, a cloud of silence descended upon me. When my first home was destroyed by the Unakas, the cloud stayed with me for many months, and it came again when Beloved Mother died, when Chera died, and when I learned of Nancy's death. The cloud did not come on this day, so I said prayers and drew the silence around me in respect to Mother Gambold.

We rode for many miles without speaking—Jonathan, Star, and I. When the sun reclined on the tops of the distant hills, though, my heart was suddenly bursting with joy and my mind was filled with bright thoughts. Star was now my charge! I was to take care of her, and it mattered not that I was young or without parents. We would be together, the two of us. I felt light and free, the way I did when Star and I had skipped across the meadow. I wanted to stop the wagon and dance along the road, but I did not want to be disrespectful to Mother Gambold, so I remained quiet, but still my spirit soared.

Star, however, had sat quietly for long enough, and she began a conversation with Jonathan about animal friends and small fish in streams and sparkling rocks. Then she asked questions about the household. She was excited to hear that we had a puppy and also two small children who were toddling about and learning words for the world around them. Jonathan described Long Fellow as a kindly grandfather, although none of us living there were his grandchildren. Five Killer was portrayed as a handsome, strong brave who had once been a fierce warrior. He would be like an uncle. Star would like Turtle Woman, the mother of the children, Jonathan assured, for Turtle was kind to everyone. Finally, Raven. I held my breath as he talked of her. Yes, Raven would be glad I was returning to attend to this matter of the "paper," but I was returning with a child and not a husband.

"What? Another orphan child in this family? And a girl?" she would complain to Five Killer. "We have no room. She and Dancing Leaf will have to find another place to live. Besides, the time has come for Dancing Leaf to move on and begin her own family." Maybe Raven would even say these things in front of Star.

We stopped for our evening meal when we reached the Ocoee River. Jonathan shot a rabbit, which I skinned and roasted on a spit over the fire. We ate bean dumplings that the Cherokee cooks at the council meeting had passed out as people departed. When we finished eating, we stretched ourselves on blankets under the cool of the shade tree. It felt good to rest our limbs, and we were all soon in the dream world.

Jonathan and I awoke early, in the gray hours before dawn had tinged the sky with red and gold. We worked quietly to gather our things, for

Star remained asleep, undisturbed by our movements. I made a pallet with the blankets for her in the back of the wagon, and Jonathan laid her down. Her eyes did not open, not even when he jostled the reins or when the wagon bounced over bumpy places in the road.

Jonathan looked back to assure himself that she was sleeping, and then he said, "There's a letter from Blue Lake waiting for you."

A letter from Blue Lake? He spoke as if it were a small, unimportant matter, but I felt as if I were Star Woman, spiraling to a new world below.

I could not talk for several minutes, and then I tried to make my voice calm as I asked, "Why did you not tell me about this before?"

He shrugged. "Guess I forgot. The other stuff—telling you about the paper from the government office, talking with the Gambolds, attending the council meeting—all these other things seemed more important."

I made no reply. I simply looked at him, and perhaps he saw in my expression how much the letter meant to me.

"I don't know why I didn't tell you, Dancing Leaf," he admitted. "Guess I should have. Sorry."

I was angry, but with Star in our presence, I did not think it wise to argue. Besides, I noticed a humbleness in Jonathan's manner that I had not seen before. In old days he would have said, "Well, what difference does it make? You'll have to wait till you get there to read the letter anyway." But he did not say this. Besides, he had done much for me in the past weeks.

We entered a wooded area, and the road narrowed. Jonathan jumped out to clear away a tree branch. When he picked up the reins again, he asked, "Do you think the letter says he's on his way back?"

That question was in my mind also, and I said, "If he has written a letter, then I don't think he will be returning. If he planned to return, then surely he would have done so by now." My voice was firm, but my heart was not.

He looked to Star once more, and still she slept. "We could get married, Dancing Leaf," he said. "You and I."

Ai-yee! Married? True, the idea had danced through my head at times, but many other matters crowded our lives. Besides, we had not followed the proper path that leads two people to marriage. How could we leap such a distance?

"Star would live with us," he continued, seeing my uncertainty. "We're young to be her parents, but my family would help out, and the others in your family, too. They would be pleased we were establishing our own homestead."

Jonathan's thoughts, I realized, had traveled much further on this road than my own.

"We could build a cabin on my father's farm. He's getting too old to work it by himself. And on Sundays I'd be preaching. The church will be for both Cherokee and whites, and with your encouragement, your people will come."

He glanced at me as he talked, but his eyes always went back to the road, which curved through the forest of trees. I allowed myself to look at him without turning away. I liked the way he sat tall on the seat and the ease with which he held the reins and called out to Red Sky when she needed direction. His shoulders were broad, his legs long, his hair golden, his face handsome. Every morning his shirt was clean, and the small black book, which meant so much to him, was always in his pocket. He was a man of God and not a man of whiskey or gambling or other such things. And he was a man who cared about my people. Plenty of white men were intent on pushing us from our land, but Jonathan was not interested in land.

"Would you not prefer to have a Unaka wife?" I asked. "And your parents also?"

"My parents loved your mother, and they will love you, too. And your family likes me—well, it seems they like me well enough. So it would be a good match all around."

"'A good match all around'? Beloved Mother answered with those very words when I asked her why she had married Bryant Ward."

"She married a white man?" Jonathan was surprised by this, but he had not known her when she was a married woman. Through marriage she acquired the name *Ward,* and the white people called her Nancy Ward.

"Yes, her first husband was Cherokee," I explained, "but she was only eighteen when he was killed in battle. Bryant Ward was a trader in the days when white people could not travel safely through Indian land, so having a Cherokee wife was a good arrangement. And the match benefited the Cherokee, too, because a white husband of a Cherokee woman could help negotiate with soldiers and other traders."

"Well, the match would be good for us, too," Jonathan encouraged. "We'd set up a family for Star. You could get away from Raven and have your own place."

"And how would this marriage benefit you?" I asked.

He opened his mouth to speak, but no words followed. He sat up taller then and cleared his throat before he answered. "I believe God's will is that I administer to your people and bring them to salvation."

"And if we married, this would be easier for you?"

"Well, for one, I don't speak Cherokee. And your people . . . well, they would surely trust me if we lived as man and wife."

"I don't know if I can be a Christian," I replied.

I could not judge his thoughts when I made that statement. He did not look at me but instead kept his steady gaze on the road before us.

And what of our feelings? The question formed in my mind, but I could not ask it. Instead I thought of Five Killer and Raven; they had magic between them. And I saw it with Talking River and Spider Woman, and Father and Mother Gambold, and Major Ridge and Susanna also. Would there be magic between Jonathan and me? For many days now we had been companions. We had not argued even once; our time had been well spent. But we did not steal away to have precious time together the way Blue Lake and I had. And I did not experience anxious moments or feelings of longing when we were apart. Perhaps these feelings would come. I raised my eyes and saw Jonathan watching me.

"You worry too much, Dancing Leaf," he said and smiled.

He placed both of the reins in one hand and extended his free arm to me, and I could not help but be drawn in. I scooted close to him and leaned against his chest. He rested his lips on the top of my head. I slipped one arm around his back and the other across his chest and squeezed gently. I thought of the many things he had done for me—

he had shot the coyote; he had arranged care for the speckled pup; he had traveled a long distance to the mission school; he had stayed with me at the council meeting until I was ready to leave. And he had never complained or argued or boasted or insisted the entire time.

Yes, it could be a good match.

We arrived home at midday. As I peered toward the cabin, I saw that only Long Fellow was sitting on the porch. He rose quickly, though, and called the others. Five Killer appeared with one twin under each arm, and Raven followed him, and then Turtle also. They shaded their eyes from the sun and looked toward us. I waved my arm back and forth the way the Unakas do, and Star mimicked me. I thought to jump off the wagon and run toward the cabin, but I wanted to be a woman in this household, not a child. And besides, no one was coming forward, although Long Fellow was off the porch and standing at the bottom of the steps.

When we reached the pine tree, though, the child in me would not be stilled, and I had Jonathan stop the wagon. He helped Star and me climb down, and the two of us joined hands and hurried to cover the remaining distance.

The speckled pup ran out to greet us, barking and nipping playfully at our heels. I could hardly believe this small creature was now running and tumbling about. Star squealed with delight and tried to pick him up. He licked her face, but he was too lively for her arms and wriggled himself free and chased us in circles as we proceeded.

When I reached Long Fellow, my eyes filled with tears, and they spilled down my cheeks as we embraced. "I have brought a guest," I informed him when we drew apart. "This is Star."

"Hello, Grandfather," she said confidently, as if she had just returned from a long trip.

He took her hand in his own and pressed it and said, "Welcome, Grandchild."

Five Killer, Turtle, Running Deer, and Little Fawn were in the yard, and I embraced each one in turn. Five Killer picked up Star and twirled her around so that she laughed.

"Ah," he said, "another beautiful woman in our home. The Creator takes care of me so well in my old age."

"But I am a little girl," Star informed him seriously.

He stopped twirling to look at her, as if he had not thought of this.

"I can help take care of you, though," she added. "I can make corn cakes. Do you like corn cakes?"

"Yes," he answered, "I like them very much."

Raven remained on the porch throughout our greetings. I had not called out to her, nor had I looked directly at her, but from the corner of my eye I could see that she stood tall, her arms crossed, her face somber. Her presence was so large and so strong that I thought we would not be able to get past her and cross the threshold into the house.

But Star did not know to be troubled by these thoughts, so she boldly mounted the steps while I watched frozen from behind. "You are Raven," she said in a voice of wonder. "You are so beautiful," she added, arcing her arms skyward to show that all of Raven was included in her statement.

For a brief second our eyes crossed paths—Raven's and mine—a look of bewilderment on both of our faces.

"I am Star," Star announced with a nod, and she waited patiently for a response.

"Star," Raven repeated. Her face was soft, for even she could not resist the charm of this small child. "What a beautiful name," she added, taking Star's hand in her own.

"Come, come," Turtle said. "You must be tired. Come inside. There are too many pesky bugs out here. I have made a cobbler of peaches. We will all sit down, and you will tell us of your adventures, Dancing Leaf."

With so many things to tell, I could not judge where to begin, so Jonathan told about the council meeting and the many people we had met. Then, when we were eating a second helping of cobbler, Raven retreated to the sleeping room and returned with a scroll of paper, which she handed to Five Killer. She nodded gravely to him as if to say, *We have waited long enough—it is time to attend to serious matters.* I noticed how thick and strong the paper was as Five Killer unrolled it. The writing was large, and the ink dark and scripted.

"Before Mother died," Five Killer announced, "she visited the government agency and registered our property in her name so that our claim to it would be recognized in the white man's world. She was given this paper, which is called a deed."

He handed the paper to me, and for a moment the only noise in the room was the sound of the paper, softly rumpling under my fingers.

My voice echoed from the walls as I read. "Nancy Ward, a native of the Cherokee Nation, did on the 19th day of November, 1818, register her name in the Cherokee Agent's Office for the section of land one mile below John McIntosh's on Mouse Creek where the Old Trace crosses said creek leading from Tellico Block House to Hiwassee Garrison. Beginning at the ford and running down said creek for a compliment conformably to a treaty between the United States and the Cherokee Nation."

I looked up to see Five Killer and Long Fellow nodding. The boundaries on the paper agreed with the ones in their minds. "This reservation," I continued, "upon her death is for diverse causes and considerations bequeathed to her beloved daughter, Dancing Leaf, and her heirs forever."

I reread the last words silently before I raised my eyes. When I did look up, Five Killer stated the thought in everyone's mind: "It seems we are all living on your land," he said quietly. His manner reminded me of Chera when she trotted through the yard with a chicken egg in her mouth. My eyes went to Long Fellow, and I wondered if he was irritated, for we all knew that he had built the cabin.

But he seemed amused, although his words were serious enough. "The agent says you are to sign the proper papers, Dancing Leaf, if we are to establish places of business or worship. We cannot continue until you sign."

"Yes, you must quickly sign." Raven rapped her knuckles next to the scroll on the table. "The work has been held up for much too long because of this silly paper."

The words came to my mind—*Yes, of course, I will sign*—but they were not on my lips. Instead I simply looked at her, as if the matter needed further consideration.

"Perhaps you did not wish to sign," she said, "because you believe, like the white man, that property belongs only to the person whose name appears on the paper." Her voice was like the steady drum of a woodpecker, and still I could not bring myself to speak. "Well, that is not the Cherokee way. We all live here together, and the land belongs to all of us. Or do you not think so?"

I did not answer, but I carefully rolled up the paper and placed it in Five Killer's hands.

"This paper talk is only a small matter," she continued, her voice now like a screechy mouse.

Dew appeared on her upper lip; I had never seen it there before. Still, I could not say the words she hoped to hear.

Instead, I said, "The paper talks of the white men are never small matters. Come," I addressed Jonathan and Five Killer, "let's walk down to the inn and see the improvements that have been made. My mind was on other business before I left, and I did not give proper attention to your plans."

I did not invite Raven to come with us, and she did not invite herself, so Jonathan and Five Killer and Star accompanied me to the bottom of the hill, where the inn rested near the Ocoee River.

It would be a handsome building, I judged, as I walked around the shell of what was to be. Fresh boards rose like cornstalks planted in rows. One house was stacked on top of the other, the same as in the mission school. The wooden doorway had been widened to the size of two large doors. I breathed in the fresh scent of the newly cut wood and wondered how trees could be so neatly stripped of bark and cut so perfectly.

"Upstairs will be three rooms," Five Killer explained. "Two for travelers who need lodging. One for Turtle and her children and her husband, should they decide to stay. We will place a counter in the old part of the inn and behind it shelves for the goods to be sold—iron cooking pots and pans, nails, hammers and tools, spun cloth, spices for cooking, all of the things that are in the white man's store—we will sell these things.

"The two rooms on the bottom level," he said as he stepped into the frame of the new construction, "will be for Raven and me. One for sleeping and the other for Raven's work—her loom and spinning wheel. She will sell the belts and dresses and turbans and other things that she makes."

"Yes, I see," I answered, turning slowly to take it all in. I liked the picture that came to my mind—visitors arriving every day. The inn would be lively with much talking and exchanging.

"And here," Five Killer said as he took my arm and we stepped onto land where no boards had been raised, "we hope to construct another building large enough for Cherokee meetings. A building that could seat at least a hundred people."

"On Sundays it'd be the house of worship," Jonathan quickly added, "for Cherokee and white people alike."

"Where will be the school?" Star asked suddenly.

All three of us turned in surprise to look at her.

She repeated, "Where will be the school?"

Still no one made a reply, so she said, "I will need to go to school, and the other children also, and even Little Deer and Running Fawn when they are old enough."

"True," I agreed, "we will need a school. And why could it not be in the meeting house? The council meets only on special occasions, and Jonathan will need it only for Sunday services. This building you speak of would be large enough for a schoolhouse."

"We'd have to get a teacher," Five Killer said, and I heard doubt in his voice.

"Dancing Leaf can be our teacher," Star replied. "Mother Gambold said she would be a fine teacher for Cherokee children."

"Yes, I could be a teacher," I echoed, as I turned and gazed about, thinking of desks and books and shelves. "We will need books for this school," I informed Five Killer. "I will speak to the white agent when I sign the papers."

"Will you teach them white man's writing or Cherokee writing?" Star asked.

"Both," I said. "And songs and stories, too. I can teach them the ones we learned at Spring Place School, but they will learn Cherokee songs and stories, too."

"And I'd preach to the children at least once a week," Jonathan said, "and teach them commandments and Bible stories."

I nodded my agreement and turned to Five Killer. "How long before a building such as this could be built?"

"It will not take long," he assured me. "Sam Walkingstick and his sons and Johnny Rainwater and his brother have agreed to help."

As we strolled back toward the cabin, I turned to Star. "You were very wise to think about the school."

"I like this place," she said. "Will it be our home?"

"Yes, this is our home. This is our family."

The day was closing, and it was too late to travel to town to sign the papers. The next day I would see to the matter. But now the other paper demanded my attention—the letter from Blue Lake. I had seen it lying on the shelf of the cupboard when I first entered the cabin. Immediately I had recognized the handwriting, but I had stilled my heart and told myself to wait.

And now I saw the letter again for the second time as I entered. I did not want the others to see my hands tremble as I opened it, so I grabbed it and slipped it under my belt and announced to the others, "I will be sitting on the rock by the stream. Jonathan, will you milk the cow so Turtle can help with the evening meal? Star, you will help with the children."

Star was delighted to be assigned this task, and Turtle's face was one of amusement that I should be making these decisions. Raven looked as if a bull had just lowered his horns and butted her from behind. I was pleased to see this look on her face. The next day I would say nothing, and Raven could make all the decisions of the house again, because these things mattered little to me. But on this day, I enjoyed feeling in charge.

I closed the door behind me and had traveled only a few steps when I heard the door close once again. The heavy footsteps I knew were Jonathan's.

"Dancing Leaf," he called.

I stopped and turned to him.

"I don't think it will work, this marriage of ours, if you can't be a

Christian." He did not sound angry or troubled. His eyes looked at me with truth, and they searched for truth in my own.

"I don't know if I can be a Christian," I replied.

He shrugged, and his next words were unsure. "I don't know about teaching these kids Cherokee songs and such in the house of God. It doesn't seem right to me."

"Ah," I said politely, for I did not wish to argue at this time. "There is much to consider, but we have plenty of time. We will discuss these matters later."

He lowered his face and scratched his ear, then smiled when he raised his eyes to me again. We both knew that many disagreements lay before us, and yet arguing did not seem such a dreadful thing. I watched as he walked back, his hands in his pockets, his shoulders squared.

I heard again Beloved Mother's words of counsel from days past: *One must learn to live with a thunder being.* I turned my eyes to Galunlati above and knew what her words would be if she could speak to me now: *Yes, one must learn to live with a thunder being, but one should not marry a thunder being.*

THE LEGEND OF THE STRAWBERRIES

Many years ago when Mother Earth was still young, the Great One created a man and woman to live in companionship and harmony. The two lived happily for a long time until one morning when the woman became very angry with the man and stomped out of their cabin.

By mid-afternoon the woman still had not returned. When the man went out to look for her, he saw her in the distance, climbing a mountain to the west. Immediately he set out after her, but she was too far away. He lifted his voice in prayer. "O Great One," he pleaded, "I love her but cannot reach her. What can I do?"

"What is the problem?" asked the Great One.

Now, this upset the man because the Great One is supposed to know everything that happens and why. Besides, the man did not know what had caused the problem, and he was so distraught, he could not think clearly.

"Are you sure you did not do anything?" asked the Great One.

"I don't know," replied the man, "but she is getting farther and farther away."

"I know that your heart is true," the Great One spoke reassuringly to the man. "I will do what I can to slow her down."

The Great One caused a huckleberry bush to spring up along the woman's path, and then a patch of blackberries, but she hurried on without even looking down. *Aha!* thought the Great One. *I must make her look down in humility before she will stop and listen to what is in her heart.* So he put a small bush on the ground with leaves that hid a luscious, sweet-smelling fruit shaped like a heart.

When the woman came to the little plant, the aroma enticed her and she knelt to see beautiful, heart-shaped berries. She let go of her anger and picked some for her husband, whom she loved with all her heart. When she saw him in the distance, she ran excitedly toward him, and they embraced for a very long time in the setting sun. She gave him the bright red strawberries, and together they gave thanks for being reunited.

Chapter 12

My pace was not hurried as I approached Grandfather Rock. In a few moments, I would read the letter from Blue Lake, and the mystery of whether he would return or not would be known. So I walked slowly, calming my heart and preparing myself to make friends with either answer.

"Ah, Grandfather Rock," I said as I seated myself. "Only three weeks have passed since I last sat here, but much has happened, and I have returned a different person." I wriggled back and forth, searching for the exact place that molded to me. Finally I found the position of comfort, but it did not feel the same as before. I was sure that Grandfather Rock felt this change also.

I took the knife attached to my belt and ran it under the waxed seal. Then I removed the thick, folded paper. Blue Lake's family was wealthy, I judged, if they could afford such paper. The ink was dark with no smudges.

Dearest Dancing Leaf,

Thank you for your kind letter. I have just now received it. I am sorry to hear of Chera's death. I have never trusted coyotes. I have also learned of Nancy's death. I am sorry that you have had to endure these sad times.

My father died only one week after my arrival here. I have inherited a small portion of his farm; the larger portion went to his widow and their children together. It was done this way so that I could live independently with my wife without bickering with the others. The land itself is beautiful—woods and streams and fields that grow tobacco. These people are kind enough, and there is always much to do.

I will write more later. I hope to hear from you again soon.

Blue Lake

A line of empty space appeared before the last few words, as if he had put the letter down and resumed writing at a later time. The ink was narrower; perhaps he had used a different pen.

My eyes searched the letter three times. Where were the words that would tell me if he was coming home or not? The first two times, I read anxiously, but on the third time, my fear turned to anger. Why had he not stated his intentions? Did he think I had no feelings about these matters? Did he not care about my feelings but only about his own?

There were many things he did not say in his letter. He did not ask about the inn we were building. He did not say he was glad I carried the crystal with me. He did not say if he wore the medicine pouch I had given him. He did not ask me if I had found my true path, nor did he talk about our two paths meeting again one day. And the words that were in the letter—the ones that talked of living with a wife—what wife would that be? Perhaps he had met a pretty Unaka girl.

I was sorry I had written the letter to him that revealed so many of my own feelings. I was too angry for sitting. I climbed down from the rock and stood.

"I do not like this letter, Blue Lake," I declared aloud. "I do not like these words. I have held you in my heart for some time, but I release you now. I am destroying your letter with the ugly words." I tore it into tiny pieces, and I dropped the pieces one by one into the water and watched them float down the stream until they were no longer visible. "This water will carry your words far away from me. And my feelings for you will be carried with them also."

Tears flowed from my eyes, but I judged them to be cleansing tears. The energy of angry feelings remained, however, and I did not wish to

176

sit or stand. I wished to walk, so I walked on the path along the stream by the light of the half-moon.

I heard the low cry of the great horned owl, and when I looked up to the hollowed tree branch, his golden eyes were fastened on me. I told the forest creatures to respect the distance between us, for I was angry and did not wish to have my path crossed by one of them. I walked with no special thoughts in mind, my moccasined feet beating a steady rhythm on the damp earth. I walked past the place where the fallen tree trunk split the water. I walked past the hollow where the shadow of twin hills appeared in the distance. I continued past the crossing where giant rocks rose like turtles' backs above the water.

When I reached the small falls, where beavers often build their dams, I stopped, for the path was covered with vines and underbrush. I leaned my back against a tree trunk and measured my breaths until they were slow and even, and then I turned and with a slower pace retraced my footsteps.

By the time I reached Grandfather Rock, the dark clouds of anger were gone and my thoughts were clear. I seated myself and gazed upward. The stars above were plainly visible, and the moon was revealing half of her face. In one week, I judged, the moon would be full, and it would be two months since Blue Lake's departure. Much had happened.

I had traveled to the mountain village where Talking River and Spider Woman removed my bad dreams. I distinctly saw these two in my mind, and I vowed that Star and I would visit them before the snows of winter descended on the mountains.

I thought of Chera's death and Nancy's death, and pain washed over me again. But the pain was not as sharp as before, and instead of Chera's stiff body, I saw her as she charged the raccoon and bravely fought the coyote. Nancy Ridge's form, too, appeared in my mind, and I saw her standing on the veranda, a child in her arms. She waved to me, and I knew that all was well.

I saw John Ridge laughing and talking as we rode in the carriage, and I heard again his words of advice. Yes, he would be a wise and powerful leader like his father.

Mother Gambold I observed in her medicine patch, retrieving plants. She turned and waved to me, and I knew her thoughts: *You must continue with your medicines, Dancing Leaf. We all will die, but the medicines will help sick people to get well and live longer.* I vowed then to gather more herbs and replenish the supply that Beloved Mother had kept. I would keep my own garden, too, like Mother Gambold, so that I might always have some on hand.

I saw Star as she had looked in the schoolhouse on the day I first met her—so serious, so intent on her purpose—and I thought of how she had laughed and skipped and played in the days since. And the speckled pup, which Star named Spot—I was glad he had survived, and I saw how he stayed by her side and how much she loved him.

I thought of Sequoyah and Ahyoka and the Cherokee writing, and I renewed my vow to teach this writing to Cherokee children.

I thought of Jonathan, how he had annoyed me with his questions and his comb and his black book. But I knew then that the god of his black book, the one to whom he prayed, was the same Great One, the Creator, to whom I addressed my prayers. Jonathan and I would not live as man and wife, but he had proved himself a true friend.

I lifted my thoughts to the Great One and thanked him for all the people he had put in my path the past two months. And I gave thanks to Grandfather Rock. My own path in life was now a clearer path, and I knew that this place was my true home.

In the weeks that followed, we were busy with many tasks. The corn ripened, and although the crop was not as large as the one we had the previous year, still we brought in many ears and placed them in the storehouse. We also harvested beans from the vines and potatoes from the earth. Pumpkin and squash continued to grow, and soon we would roast them.

In the late afternoons, Star and I practiced Cherokee writing. I rewrote many of the stories I had recorded in English, and the Cherokee symbols for sounds now came easily to me. We taught Turtle also to do this writing, and she practiced with us when the small ones took their naps. Raven, of course, did not think it such a great thing, but she busied herself with her loom and sewing in the afternoons, and so the cabin was full of peaceful activity.

The nights lengthened and the days grew cooler and shorter. The afternoon sky was a dome of clear blue. The sound of hammers rang out, and soon the buildings of the inn and the meeting place were accomplished.

On the first day of the harvest moon, Raven and Five Killer and Turtle and the twins moved their belongings into the rooms of the inn. The members of the Cherokee district council came to see our improvements, and they agreed to send desks so that I might begin a school.

The "girl with the hair of fire," as Star called her, came to visit Jonathan one day. Her eyes were green, the color of spring water, and she had freckles scattered across her nose and cheeks. She stopped to ask for Jonathan, and we watched as she made her way to where he worked on benches for the meeting house. The two of them spread a blanket and sat under the tree and ate buttered bread and other things she pulled from the basket.

I heard Raven's words in my mind: *Dancing Leaf has let another one go.* But I felt only a little sadness; I knew it was not meant for Jonathan and me to be together.

While Star and I continued to watch Jonathan and this girl with red hair, Five Killer crossed our path. In one hand he had a string of fish and in the other a fistful of blackberries. He nibbled on berries as he walked.

"Where did you find such large berries?" I asked, and he told me of the bushes that grew along the road on the other side of the hill where Beloved Mother was buried.

Star and I retrieved our baskets, and we were there soon enough, putting as many blackberries into our mouths as we put into the baskets. Our lips were stained blue-purple and our fingers also. Star's small fingers were scratched from the thorns, but she didn't seem to mind.

When our baskets were full, we took a different path home that led us past the hill of the butterflies, as Star called it, for beautiful wings fluttered above the many flowers swaying in the breeze on this hill. We skipped along merrily and sang songs we had learned at the mission school.

It was Star who first detected the sweet smell and saw small, red forms. "What are these plants at our feet?" she asked.

"It's a strawberry patch," I answered, bending down to observe. Scattered on the vines were large, heart-shaped berries. "We gathered some from this very spot last spring. It surprises me to see more here now."

We busied ourselves, gathering them, but our baskets were full. So we made a pouch with my apron, and I held the two corners together as we continued on the trail to the cabin.

When we turned at the large pine tree and started down the lane, Spot came charging to greet us. Another dog was with him, and the two of them barked happily as they raced past.

My legs stopped skipping when I saw the second dog, and instead it was my heart that was skipping inside my chest, for the dog was Blackie. When I looked toward the cabin, I saw Blue Lake's horse tied to the post. I squinted my eyes as the figure stepped off the porch and began walking toward us.

"It is Blue Lake," I said to Star, but by that time, the dogs had circled around us and charged back toward the cabin. Star ran chasing after them, laughing and shouting as she went. "Don't spill your basket," I called after her.

She stopped when she reached Blue Lake, and she handed him a blackberry from her basket and then went racing on, as if she had known him all her life and could not be bothered to stop and talk.

I held my basket of blackberries in one hand and the corners of my apron with the strawberries in the other, and for a moment I stood rooted to the spot. I could not have run forward even if I had wanted. Blue Lake did not run either, but he came forward quickly enough in his easy stride. He pants were buckskin breeches, not the Unaka clothes he had probably worn in Virginia. His hair had been cut shorter, so that it hung just below his ears. He wore the blue turban that matched his eyes.

I wondered how I looked to him. Had I changed? I pressed my sticky lips together and wished they were not stained with berry juice. I wished also that I could comb my hair, for it hung loosely down my back and was not plaited. We came face-to-face, and a moment of silence passed between us.

"It is good to see you, Dancing Leaf," Blue Lake began softly. He peered into my apron. "Where did you find strawberries this time of year?"

"The Creator put them in my path." The words spilled out without thought. I put the basket down and took a strawberry from my apron and held it to him. He took a bite and then raised his hand and put the last bite into my own mouth.

I reached to my apron to remove another strawberry, but he stepped around me and carefully undid the apron ties behind my back, and he laid the apron aside and then the basket. He put his arms under mine, and he twirled me in a full circle in the way that Five Killer twirls the ones he loves.

And when we were finished laughing and twirling, I picked up the apron and he picked up the basket. We joined our free hands and walked slowly toward the cabin, where everyone—Five Killer, Raven, Running Deer, Little Fawn, Turtle, Long Fellow, and Star—stood waiting on the porch. None of them were sitting, nor were any of them talking or engaged in any other activities.

They watched silently as we approached, and they did not turn their eyes from us until they saw the smiles on our faces, and then suddenly they were all in motion. Raven grabbed the straw broom and began sweeping the steps. Turtle took the small ones by the hand and retreated into the cabin. Long Fellow leaned back in his chair and lit his pipe. Five Killer and Star stepped into the yard and threw sticks for the dogs to retrieve.

We talked for many hours that evening—Blue Lake and I—as we sat together on Grandfather Rock. I told him of my travels and of how Star had seen the morning star rising above the clear blue lake in the crystal light. I showed him my stories in Cherokee writing and talked of my plans for the school.

"Dancing Leaf," he said, as I leaned against his chest and his arms encircled mine, "the sadness that gnawed a large hole in your center and caused you much unhappiness—it is no longer there." He told me then of Virginia and the land he had sold to his half brother and of the loneliness he felt.

When we heard footsteps from behind, we turned to see who was approaching. It was Star.

"When are you coming back to the cabin?" she asked.

"Soon," I answered, and Blue Lake reached out and lifted her so that we were all three sitting on Grandfather Rock, cradled in each other's arms, with a full moon and a blanket of stars stretched above.

Two ceremonies of marriage were performed. The first was held inside the newly built meeting house. I wore the blue dress that Raven made for this special occasion and also the white doeskin moccasins that belonged to Beloved Mother. Blue Lake wore a shirt of matching blue, with ribbons of red and white sewn across the front. Jonathan stood before us and read the words from his black book, and then he made the pronouncement that we were man and wife.

We rode in wagons to the hill in the distance where Beloved Mother's grave rested. At the top of the hill, a canvas had been stretched between tall poles. In the center of the pavilion a sacred fire burned. It had been constructed from seven woods to honor the seven clans of our tribe.

Blue Lake took his place at the eastern side of the pavilion, with Five Killer standing behind him. I stood across from them on the western edge, with Long Fellow and Raven behind me. Around our shoulders we wore blue blankets. Lame Deer, the adawehi, nodded, and Blue Lake and I approached the fire from our separate directions.

Lame Deer muttered ancient words as he sprinkled tobacco into the fire. He then handed us the marriage cup filled with dried corn and water. Blue Lake and I drank from it in turn four times as we faced the directions—east, west, north, and south—declaring our union to all sides of the earth. Lame Deer took the cup, and he drank up, toward Galunlati, and down, toward Mother Earth.

I turned to Raven, who handed me the basket of corn bread, and Blue Lake turned to Five Killer, who handed him the basket of cured venison. Blue Lake and I exchanged baskets, and Five Killer and Raven came forward and removed the blue blankets from our shoulders.

Lame Deer declared in a loud voice for all to hear, "You are now departing your separate worlds of two, where the blue of loneliness and unhappiness has been upon you." He draped a blanket of white around our shoulders. "You are now united under the white blanket of happiness," he affirmed, "and so it will be for yourselves and for your children to come."

Blue Lake and I turned to each other then and exchanged the sacred words of promise. Blue Lake spoke first; my words echoed his.

"I am never lonely with you."

"I am never lonely with you."

"Your soul has come to the center of my soul, never to turn away."

"My soul has come to the center of your soul, never to turn away."

"Together we walk the white road of happiness."

"Forever we walk the white road of happiness."

The afternoon was spent with feasting and dancing, for many of our friends from neighboring villages were present.

Blue Lake and I took the bouquet of flowers I had carried during the ceremony in the meeting house and placed it on the grave of Beloved Mother. Only one tree stood on this hill, and it rose tall and stately above her grave. When I looked up into the tree, I saw the leaves of green and gold and red gently dancing in the wind. And I knew that Beloved Mother herself was dancing with joy on this day in Galunlati above. Blue Lake and I clasped hands and joined the dance of the leaves.

Star and the other children saw us and ran to join us. We were then a waving line of clasped hands and dancing feet, and we gathered others as we made our way across the hilltop. We danced north to south and east to west, and west to east and south to north, and we continued in this way until we had to stop for breath. And then we danced some more.